Petals on the Concrete

Petals on the Concrete

G. I. Wu

Rev. date: 07/31/2017

To order additional copies of this book, contact:
Xlibris
1-888-795-4274
www.Xlibris.com
Orders@Xlibris.com
761230

Acknowledgements

Where would I be without my creator? The thoughts that come to mind are not as pleasant as my life is with Him. Thank you Lord for the strength, creativity, and diligence! There isn't much I can write here that isn't expressed in the book because You claim its purpose.

I would like to thank my mother for inspiring me and teaching me the right way; even in your absence. You are the friend everyone wishes they had.

Love and appreciation for my family- this includes every last one of you! Since you have not only shown me love in my days, you have shown love to my mother and have contributed to much of her happiness; for that I am forever grateful.

Last but not least I would like to thank ALL of my supporters! I pray this book helps you in more ways than I have expected. Let me know your thoughts. I want to hear from you.~G.I WU

To: my creator

For it was you who formed my inward parts; you knit me together in my mother's womb. I praise you, for I am fearfully and wonderfully made. Wonderful are your works; that I know very well. My frame was not hidden from you, when I was being made in secret, intricately woven in the depths of the earth. Your eyes beheld my unformed substance. In your book were written all the days formed for me; when none of them existed.

Psalm 139:13-16

Chapter 1

"That's it!" Mya screamed out in frustration. She had been calling Antonio, her on again- off again boyfriend of 2 years, for a week and got so acquainted with his voicemail she started to think of the worst. "Oh you aint got time for me, hu?" She spoke unconsciously, which was a habit of hers she quickly reminded herself to get rid of. *Mya chill* she thought, *you know damn well Antonio just got that new job. If he could he'd be all over you right now.* "True" she said to herself, "except he isn't". Mya could not fully accept the fact that Antonio was a loyal boyfriend. The guys she used to devote her time to would end up using her like a toilet; and you can bet she felt like shit every time she caught one of them interested in another woman. Although Antonio was different and proved his loyalty to her more than her fingers could count, she grew weary when he missed her calls. She tried everything she could have. Besides a simple call or text message there was twitter and snapchat, the apps he used often; yet nada. She threw her phone and it landed at the end of her full side mattress dressed in her favorite cheetah print comforter. As more horrific thoughts seeped through her conscious she wonder why she put up with this foolishness and questioned her relationship with Antonio.

They met 3 years ago both freshmen in college. Although they were new friends, She still felt a connection with him. A connection that words could not express unless the oxford dictionary would accept aldjfhgakg. This connection was so strong she could not believe that Antonio was responsible for such an indescribable feeling because during their 2 year long friendship, she never thought they'd be more than friends. Plus, he had been dating his high school sweet heart and was madly in love; until he found out she cheated on him. Mya, being his backbone, helped him piece his heart back together and they found themselves in love ever since. He was everything she dreamed of in a guy, a good sense of humor, intelligence, good looks, compassion, and most importantly God in his life. She knew his main goal was to maintain and she loved how much he supported his family, even if they were the reason he was always busy. Mya sighed. She missed him, but not more than she missed her mother who died when Mya was nine; 12 years ago. It is crazy how fast time flies. It seemed just yesterday that she was getting ready for her first day of freshman year of college. Now, here she is closer to graduation and so ready to get on with her life. A life she and Antonio could finally share together. After their freshman year he was forced to drop out of school for failure to afford it. His parents got caught up in their own personal issues after their divorce. Unfortunately, he was tied into it along with his two younger siblings; Tobias and Luis. This caused him to sacrifice his goals instead and keep his little brothers in line. He lived back home alternating between his mother's and father's home in Lansing, Illinois. Mya was six hours away in a small town called Carbondale, Illinois attending Southern Illinois University working toward her undergraduate degree in Spanish Education. In their last conversation, they both decided once Mya graduated she would attend graduate school near him. That was another reason she desperately wanted to talk with him, to make sure they were still on the same page.

Her phone vibrated, indicating an incoming call. She rushed to reveal the screen praying it was Antonio returning her call. Her heart raced with joy but instantly dropped when her father's name and picture lit up on her Iphone 4s. She talked with her father answering the same questions he asked every conversation: How's school? You doing alright? Finish your homework? And her favorite, Where's that boy at? "Good. Yes. Yes; and what boy daddy? She responded and they shared a laugh. "Good, that makes daddy very happy! You tell that boy I got a gun and I'm not afraid to use it or go to jail." Her father laughed afterwards, but Mya knew that he meant every word until death do them part. "I love you daddy." She said redirecting the conversation. "Daddy loves you too." He blew a kiss through the phone. After she returned one, they ended the call. She enjoyed those talks with her father except like the ones she shared with Antonio, they didn't last long enough. Her father, an officer for a hospital in St Louis, Missouri worked 12 hour shifts a day; so she really cherished the fact he took time off to touch base with her. She glanced over at the clock that told her it was way past her bed time. It took her some time to fall asleep so she liked to be in bed by 9 p.m. and here it was already 11 p.m. Realizing she couldn't wait around for Antonio's call any longer, she plugged the charger in the phone, set it on the nightstand, wrapped the covers over her blue satin pajamas and fell asleep.

Antonio unplugged his phone from the charger. He rolled his eyes once he saw Mya called him again. *What is wrong with this girl, can a nigga get some space?* With his mood altered he turned his phone to airplane mode and placed it on the iHome speakers Mya bought him. Drake's *So Far Gone* album bumped through the speakers. Now all that was left was to roll up a joint. After working overtime for the last four nights and babysitting his little brother Luis after school, he was exhausted and Maryjane was his trusted companion in times like this. The next song "Karaoke" played and Antonio lit the joint, inhaled the solution, and then exhaled the bullshit. This weekend was rough to him, what he could use other than what he already enjoyed at this moment was a back massage from Mya. Since he couldn't call her up to get one, there was no point in calling her at all. She would only nag him about not returning her calls, which would elevate the anger he already had stirred up within. Most of his problems he didn't find worth sharing. If he couldn't solve them, no other man could. Nevertheless, it was in God's will; He trusted that He was the all-knowing and had the final say. Antonio recited the words feeling Drake's, Karaoke. It reminded him of his ex and Mya at the same time. He loved Mya- would give her the clothes off his back if she needed them; rain or shine. She had been there for him at his lowest point and stayed encouraging through tough times. He would never do anything to hurt her nor mistreat her because his heart only had one beat, and her name was written all over it. As much as he loved her and their deep conversations, he needed alone time which was what he enjoyed right now. No list of demands, no interrogations, and no heavy lifting; it was about time. Antonio felt the weed kicking in soon as he pulled the roach away from his lips. He exhaled and returned the roach to the ashtray. Then he hopped in the shower, got in bed, and fell asleep as soon as his cheek met the pillow.

Mya tossed and turned frustrated to get comfortable in bed. After what seemed like hours of playing Russian roulette with her sleep, she pulled out her bible finding the folded sheet of paper she saved in the book of Daniel 2:20. She opened it and read down the list, smiling at each heart felt message she recorded. They were phrases that Antonio said to her. She wrote them down as love reminders. It was her way of putting her mind at ease from thinking their relationship was failing. Before she could completely read the last phrase, she dozed off with the paper held tightly in her right hand.

Chapter 2

The sky was a dark red. The white moon resembled the smile of a Cheshire cat. The clouds were thick like a mustache. Mya was cold, wearing a small biker jacket with leggings. She couldn't understand why she was outside without wearing shoes, or a heavier coat for that matter. She was hesitantly looking around as if she were searching for an answer in the fog. Nothing, not a sound was heard nor a familiar face seen. Her body led her to a house as if she were under a spell. She casually walked up the steps to enter the opened door. Bam! Something struck her with force so hard and quick she didn't realize what happened or how she ended up before the steps again. She repeated the first action and well just as before, BAM! Something struck her. She fell back and stayed there helplessly. Suddenly, a figure ran toward her. Her heart met her stomach and her eyes met her forehead, when she realized this was no savior. This man had a knife. This man was coming for her! There was no better time for her legs to go numb. As the white man stood inches away from her, her heart pounded furiously making it hard for her to catch her breath. Please! Help... HELP!" She mouthed; her words mute. The white man caressed her body inappropriately with the knife held to her throat. Without saying a word, he unzipped her jacket and forced himself on top of her. Mya closed her eyes and silently prayed. KNOCK! KNOCK! She kept hearing and finally realized they were coming from the outside world; reality. She rushed out from her reoccurring nightmare that still seemed too real for comfort. Turning over to face the door, she responded to her roommate. "Come in Sherry." Sherry slowly opened the door and poked her head through the opening revealing her blue-green eyes. "Good Morning, Lover!" She sang. "Good Morning." Mya groaned. "Are you okay? I heard you saying something." She was concerned. Mya sighed unable to reveal the truth about what she'd experienced a few minutes prior. "Yeah, I'm okay. Thanks for checking." She smiled hoping that she'd pacified Sherry well enough. "Good. I thought you were calling me. Anyways its 7:15 now, I know you have to be a work at 8. So, I'll let you get ready." Shocked to hear she slept through her 7 a.m. alarm Mya hopped up to pick an outfit for the day. Once she decided that the brown oxfords looked better with the plain teal dress shirt and dark blue jeans, she matched it with her feather earrings, the same color as her shirt, and black watch. Like every morning, she headed to the bathroom before getting dressed. She faced the mirror expecting to see a black eye but nothing; same old chocolate skin, brown wide eyes, round nose, and puckered lips. Mya was a breath-snatching-neck-breaking woman, so she believed. Finding that she was spending more time than she had in the mirror, she continued her morning routine with her thoughts spent on the nightmare. Mya placed the earring in her left ear completely ready to go. One final check in the mirror, she smiled agreeing that her butt looked the bomb in her favorite jeans. Once she heard Tony, Sherry's boy toy, enter their home she knew she best be on her way. "Bye Sherry!" She hollered shutting the door behind her, but she was too distracted by Tony to reply.

Mya sat at the front desk eating a bagel at work. It was Tuesday which meant she was working job number 2 in the Africana Studies department eight until 12 pm today. Before Antonio started working that new job he would call her every morning on this day. Though it had been almost a month since then, it was still something she was trying to get used to. She reached into her backpack to find her daily planner to revive the assigned homework due later that day. "Español trescientosviente A," She read out loud to practice her pronunciation "Ejercicio A y B." She opened her textbook then got straight to it. This week's lesson was demonstratives: this, that, these, and those. As she finished up the last bite of her bagel her cellphone sang Kendrick Lamar's Poetic Justice, reminding her to change her phone to silent and that Antonio was calling her. *Bout time!* She slid the green bar to answer and plugged one headphone in her left ear. "Was good lil homie?" Antonio sounded high as usual. Mya rolled her eyes obviously upset. "Hello." She said pretending to sound distracted by her work. Antonio let out puff of thick smoke and brought the blunt back to his thick caramel lips. "What you doing?" He held the smoke in. "What I'm always doing at 8:30 in the morning; at work." Mya spat. She didn't like acting so cold toward him, but she didn't like thinking he was ignoring her either. The cold shoulder was a defense mechanism to prove she wasn't desperately waiting for his call though they both knew she was. "Mmm." Antonio responded ignoring her tone. "Shit... don't let me bother you." Mya's heart felt heavy. *Damn. How does he do that?* Antonio was good at pulling her out of that mood he knew was a front. Plus, he didn't have time to argue about missing calls like they were high school lovers. They both were grown trying to maintain an adult life style, there was no time for pettiness; especially in a relationship. Mya sighed letting go of her grudge and invisible shield between them. "You know you're not bothering me, I was only upset about you missing my calls." She revealed. "I know Mya. Relax G. You know I'm out here grinding." "On who?" Mya joked. Antonio couldn't help but laugh at her humor that had some hidden insecurities. "On Franny and Annie." He joked talking about the dead presidents: Benjamin Franklin and Andrew Jackson. Mya laughed catching onto his humor as well. "How you been baby?" Her tone softened. "I'm straight." He responded, as if straight summed it all up. Mya rolled her eyes hating that answer but she hoped it meant his life was on the right track so that they could live out the life they'd planned. She thought about making that the next topic of discussion when Antonio interrupted her before she could speak. "Hey Mya..." He said in his sweet angelic tone and she knew what he was going to say next. She sighed confirming that their conversation was soon coming to an end. "I love you." He sang in the same tone. "I love you too." She said disappointed "Give me a kiss." Antonio spoke to her as if she was five. "Mwah" She blew one to him through the phone and he smiled and blew one back, then hung up. Mya returned to her school work fighting the urge to think about him.

Sitting in her last class of the day, Non-Violent communication, she couldn't help but ignore the teacher. Though she enjoyed this class over any other, her mind was stuck on her nightmare since she noticed the white man from her dream resembled the same white man that sat across from her in class. He raised his hand to answer a question the teacher had asked.

She praised him, approving his response. Since then, Mya replayed the attack over and over. The hands on the clock motioned that class was over. As the rest of the students gathered their things and headed out quicker than they arrived, Mya's teacher waved her over to the desk where she sat. "I noticed you and I barely made eye contact this evening." Mya always paid attention in the class and often times shared a smile or laugh with Mrs. Marie. They favored each other so this was something out of the ordinary. "Is everything alright?" She asked with a look of concern in her green eyes. Mya fought back the tears and hung her head in case one broke through. "Yes. I'm really tired." Responding with a smile, Mya lifted her head up to convince her teacher it was true. Without speaking another word, she and her teacher shared a warm embrace and Mya was touched to receive such empathy. She wasn't ready to discuss the evil her mind contained but a hug was something that eased the pain. Feeling the tears grown heavy on her eyes again, Mya sighed and they freed one another. "See you Thursday!" Mya said with a fake smile and a wave then headed out of the classroom. She was surprised to see that her friend, Riley, was waiting for her in the hallway. "Hey!" She revealed her brilliant smile that made her almond skin glow. "Awww you waited for me." Mya smiled. "What you want?" She joked. "Woah!" Riley shot back playing along, "Listen, I wanted to know if you want to go shopping this weekend. Payday is this Friday." Riley could've been Mya's left hand and Mya could've been her right, they were so in sync with one another especially when they enjoyed spending a day shopping. Mya could not relate to anyone else in Carbondale the way she related to Riley and she thought the same. "I don't even know why you asked," Mya laughed. "You know I'm always down to go bankrupt with you." "Great!" Riley said laughing. "Well Mocha," She called Mya by her nickname, "I shall see you Thursday and then this weekend." "You shall" The two breath taking women sashayed out the door. Riley headed to her next class while Mya went the opposite way home. She was relieved her day was over with and tried not to think about the nightmare or the fact she had to do it all over again.

Antonio rolled over turning off his 3:30 alarm. The sun was shining so there was no need to burn electricity by turning on the light. He grunted and yawned. He'd been sleeping since he got off the phone with Mya that morning. Happy to see that she didn't call gave him the impression she was satisfied with their conversation. The rumbling in his stomach notified him it was time to eat and soon because work began at 6. He got dressed for work and then headed out the door; his first stop was to pick Luis up from school. "Wassup Louie." He greeted his little brother. "Hi Antonio" He replied in a low tone and buckled up his seat belt in the back. "How was school?" Antonio asked before driving off. "Alright." He shrugged his shoulders. "Why don't you hop in the front seat with me?" Routinely, Luis knew better to ride in the back, their mother ruled it was safer because he is ten years old. So, Antonio hoped this would lift his little brother's spirit up a bit. "Really?" He grew excited. Antonio faced him nodding his head. Luis rushed from the back seat and plopped down in the front. He buckled up for safety and met his dark brown eyes with his eldest brother. "What about mom?" He didn't want to get in trouble and Antonio sensed that. "I'll handle mom, if she finds out." He smiled, hinting that his position as co-pilot would be their little secret. Luis laughed and shared his day at school with Antonio, his best friend. They stopped at Burger King on the way to the house when Luis decided he was content enough with riding in the back seat as protocol. Antonio arrived at home, dropped Luis off, and drove off as soon as their mother waved confirming Luis wasn't alone. He was glad because some days he had to stay with him and he couldn't afford to miss any days off from his new job. As general manager of an electricity company he dealt with a variety of people, most of whom he could not stand. They were immature and constantly needing his guidance around the office. Antonio enjoyed holding such a high position although, some days he found himself completing task the other employees were assigned. In no rush to get to work he studied the digital clock on the car radio and relaxed when it told him that he had enough time to smoke with his friend Carol.

"What you know bout that?" Antonio revealed a tightly rolled joint. "You were probably up all night on YouTube looking up how to videos." She laughed. "Fuck off." He joked. Sealing the joint she had in her hand, Carol matched Antonio and the session began. She spoke in between puffs. "How is Mya?" "Crazy." Antonio laughed and took the joint from her. "Good, you need a crazy girl." Carol said seriously. "What?" Antonio was confused. "Crazy girls know how to keep a man in line. You can't be with a girl that's too passive. You need somebody that you gotta put in their place.

You know remind them who the boss is. Helps build a man's ego." Antonio was dumbfounded he couldn't believe how much truth Carol was speaking. "My ego's already big as it is. I don't need any more fuel." Antonio played devil's advocate as always. Carol rolled her blue eyes and flipped her long dark brown hair away from her pale cheek. "Whatever; If that's the case, she wouldn't be in the picture" "True. You know I won't put up with too much bullshit." He agreed. "I'm sure it's hard for her since y'all are so far away; remember that. Shit if I were her, I'd be so sexually frustrated. I couldn't do it." Her comment made Antonio think for a moment. How did Mya do it? He knew there were thousands of guys on that campus drooling for his woman. He knew how a man's mind worked. All a woman had to do was say yes. He inhaled the smoke and blew it through his nose. "That's cause you a therm." He flicked the ashes from the joint and passed it to Carol. She forced up her middle finger and inhaled the weed. They carried on their conversation and session until both joints disappeared and they'd reached their level. Antonio had 45 minutes left in order to make it on time which was enough since it took him 20 minutes to get there.

Chapter 3

Antonio checked himself out in the mirror of the sun visor. He was blowed; he was also general manager so the former didn't matter too much. His mind drifted back to the conversation he had with Carol. He pulled out his phone about to call Mya when an unknown number popped up on the screen. "Hello?" He questioned. "Hello Antonio." A conniving voice responded from the other end. Antonio was furious. "Janet?" "Awww you remember my voice" His ex-girlfriend chimed. "All snakes hiss the same." He shot. She laughed pretending to ignore his comment and carried on the conversation. "How come you don't visit anymore?" She questioned in a baby voice that used to get her what she wanted from him. "Janet you know I have a girlfriend." She was killing his vibe and he wanted to hang up the phone, but out of respect he waited until she'd finished. It was obvious his reminder was like a bullet to the heart and Janet tried her hardest to formulate better words. "Fuck that bitch." She spat regretting them faster than she said them. Antonio laughed, "I plan to" he retorted. "In fact she is waitin for this dick right now." "Antonio I know you lying!" Janet called his bluff; there was no way in hell Mya was near while he was on the phone with another woman. "I know you not with that bitch right now, otherwise you wouldn't have answered." She was angry. "Janet, watch how you talk about my girlfriend and know that she is not as insecure as you were. Trust, I do what I want I'm Antonio mother fuckin' Gabino." Janet was speechless, and jealous of his new found love. She thought for sure those sexual nights they shared just months before Antonio and Mya got back together would be a turning point for their relationship to blossom again. Yes, Antonio regretted every second he spent using Janet as a rebound, ironically he didn't trust anybody else; especially enough to have sex with. Antonio continued. "Now, I'm bout to hang up because I can't keep her waiting any longer." He kept the story going. "You have a good night." He pulled the phone from his ear. Janet hollered but her words went unheard then it was too late, Antonio disconnected the call. Their conversation spent up most of the free time he had. He quickly returned his phone to airplane mode and slipped it in his pocket. Before getting out of his black Porsche, he fixed his green tie on his grey button down. Once he looked the part, he walked up to the building of Emerson Electricity.

As soon as he was settled in his office, he reviewed his schedule and just as he suspected it was full of jobs the other employees were to handle. Speaking of the other employees, none of them had arrived yet. This was typical yet unacceptable to Antonio. He buzzed the front desk and told the secretary Kim, to send every employee to the conference room as soon as they walked through the door. It was time to take care of business; enough was enough. Doing as she was told she relayed the message to the three men that walked in holding coffee in their hands laughing at a joke. "Thanks sexy." A tall tan man with a beard said to Kim. She scrunched her nose in disgust, though she was used to those remarks from him even if they made her uncomfortable at work. She reminded herself to speak with Antonio about his inappropriate behavior later and got back to work. The three men entered the conference room, took their seats, and talked amongst themselves. As Antonio approached the room he could hear them talking about Kim. "Man if I don't wake up with morning wood because of her. I have never seen a black woman so gorgeous in my life." The bearded man sucked his teeth recalling his sexual fantasies. "Yeah I love my wife, but I'd love her even more if she agreed to a threesome." Another guy spoke. He was cleaning his yellow teeth forcing out a piece of steak his wife cooked him. The last guy sat at the head of the table unable to reveal his thoughts about the secretary. He had a bit more respect for her than the other two. In fact he wanted a relationship with Kim and not just some platonic relationship. He dreamed of dinner by candle light and love making all night long. He raised his eyebrows when his green eyes met Antonio's brown eyes as he entered the room. Jacob the guy with the beard greeted Antonio on sight. "Gabino! How's it going?" "Mister...

Gabino" Antonio corrected him. Jacob rolled his eyes and his partner in crime, Mike, ridiculed him. "Hello Mr. Gabino." Antonio ignored the childish behavior and motioned Charles to pick another seat. Charles chose the seat to the left next to Jacob. Jacob patted him on the back. "What's this all about?" Mike asked still struggling to remove the steak from his mouth. Antonio sighed in frustration. His high was wearing off and he regretted calling this meeting mainly after Janet called him. "I called this meeting to discuss a few things." He pulled out an outline from a manila folder in his right hand. He read the points off in the order listed. "Performance, this month's duties, and lastly behavior." After catching some of their conversation earlier, he wanted to start with behavior but thought it was best to follow the outline. The men sat waiting for Antonio to continue. Antonio contemplated the best way to explain his frustration with his employee's performance. With no luck he chose to give it to them straight up. "I'm getting fed up with how much y'all been slacking on the job." Mike laughed at Antonio's choice of words. "Is there something funny Mr. Polanski?" Antonio glared at him. "Y'all" Mike repeated and Jacob joined in laughing. Charles could tell Antonio was serious and felt bad about not meeting the standards of the job. He'd been working there six months longer than Antonio had, however that didn't matter, he was the boss of all three of them. Charles respected that. Brushing off the snarky remarks, Antonio pulled out yet another mysterious paper. "This is a timesheet." He held it high for everyone to see. "A record of each of your hours and completed task," He passed three copies to his left and they circled around until Mike held the last one in his hand. Antonio cleared his throat. "As you can see, there isn't much to record. So I'm creating deadlines for the projects listed below the time chart." Each of them took heed to the paper they held in their hands. "This is ridiculous!" Mike was the first one to react. "How in the hell am I supposed to finish a month's data report in two days?" "I recommend you get started as soon as this meeting is over." Mike threw his paper down on the table and looked away from Antonio. "That's not possible, we only work six hours a day!" Jacob whined. "Then, I suggest you switch to the morning shift. I know there's an opening for your position to work 7:30am until 4:30pm. I can talk to the morning manager if you'd like" Unable to retort, Jacob stayed in the place Antonio put him in and remained silent. "No? Very well then.

Charles, do you have any comments." He questioned noticing Charles had not said a word since the meeting began. Charles shook his head no while looking down at the paper rereading his list of duties. Antonio referred to his first sheet. "Ahhh... behavior." Antonio leaned back in his chair but kept his eyes fixed on Mike who refused to face him. "There are numerous complaints about the behavior of the evening staff." "Like what?" Jacob interrupted unable to believe the words coming from Antonio's mouth. Antonio couldn't understand how these men pretended to be so unaware. "Our customers have reviewed that most of you are rude when handling technical difficulties, scheduling appointments, and payment plans. Just to name a few." He added. "We're rude? That's a lie! Those customers call us so pissed off." Jacob was so aggravated he could barely form his sentences. "Do you know... How many times I have been cursed out in one day?" Mike nodded his head in agreement. Antonio raised his hand denying Jacobs' claim. "Regardless if the customer themselves are rude or not, it is your responsibility to handle any situation properly. Remember you represent this company, like it or not!" Antonio beat the oak wood table silencing him. "Lastly, the sexual harassment complaints I've been receiving are not a good look for any one." He said; even though no reports had been filed. Mike's eyes shot open knowing he was the number one target to this issue. "There's only one woman on this job! Nobody even talks to her." He spat. "Yeah all she does is sit at the front desk all day and we sit at ours." Charles said his first words. Any other day Antonio would have believed the lies they told but he remembered what he overheard which advised him not to. "I don't believe this bullshit." Mike had enough of the mockeries. "Yeah where are these complaints?" Jacob lifted both hands to symbol air quotes. "ENOUGH!" Antonio shouted so loud it caught everyone off guard including Kim at the front desk. "I don't need to show any reports, the proof is in the pudding." He said willing to reveal his secret. "I heard you all discussing your wet dreams about Kim. I don't think it's appropriate. She is the only woman working here, both morning and evening. She is highly qualified at what she does and should simply be praised for that. It is time you all start showing her some respect around here and soon before it cost you a job and a lawsuit." Antonio organized the two white sheets of paper then, returned them to the manila folder. "Oh don't act like you're mister goody two shoes. You and all the men in here know how you really feel about Kim." Mike said trying to dig into Antonio's subconscious. "Gentlemen, I would love to argue about this now since we're already on the topic. However, I know you have tons of work due by the end of this week and it's already Tuesday. I'm going to let you get to it. Meeting adjourned." He pounded the desk with his fist as if it were a gavel and casually walked out of the conference room while the men sat there in rage.

Chapter 4

Mya was enjoying a glass of wine with the chicken Alfredo pasta she prepared for dinner. It was an ordinary Tuesday night without Antonio. Sherry was locked away in her bedroom doing her homework. Mya didn't mind the quiet. In fact, she enjoyed it. She laughed out loud at an episode of "Living Single"; episode 1 of season 5 to be exact: "Love Don't Live Here Anymore", an episode featuring love, laughter, and unfortunately disaster. Kyle purchases a one-way ticket for Max in the hopes of persuading her to move to London with him. Max is furious that Kyle will not stay in New York for her and accuses him of attempting to turn her into a housewife.

Mya took a bite of pasta from her fork trying her hardest to keep it down while focusing on the episode. As she did with every relationship she saw on t.v. or read about, Mya related them to her own. As thrilled as she would be to marry a man so financially stable she wouldn't have to lift a finger, Mya contemplated if she could spend the rest of her life that way. She aspired to travel the world and inspire the youth to beat the negative statistics and love thy neighbor as thy love themselves; a verse that kept her calm and compassionate with others. As she watched the ending credits that highlighted bloopers from the show, she anticipated for the: *to be continue...* episode to come on next. Instead an episode of "Martin" played on the screen. Mya grabbed her empty plate and took it to the kitchen. She rinsed the little that remained and placed it in the dishwasher. The oven clock showed 8:30pm. Mya wiped the area where she ate and the kitchen counter. The idis finally kicked in. Boy was she exhausted. She applied the Bath and Body Work's lotion on her body after the steamy hot shower she took. She finished with her left arm and rubbed the remaining between her hands. The satin sleepwear she wore felt so good on her delicate skin. Before going to bed she checked her email, Facebook, and blog site as if she wasn't disappointed there wasn't a sign from Antonio. Casting the first stone, she sent him a sweet good night text, and then set the phone on the magenta night stand. This time it was easy for her to fall asleep and she was out like a light.

Antonio called Mya from his work phone but failed to get a response. He returned the receiver to its place. He sat at his desk mind heavy, rubbing his eyes. With his high officially gone, he was tired.

Charles threw his head back trying to relieve the tension in his neck. He was not certain if he strained it while carrying his son's casket two weeks ago or if it was the way he was sleeping in bed; that is when he did get some sleep. He gave the list of demands one final look then continued at work. Unaware how he would complete everything by Friday, Charles grew stressed. He figured this was going to be a long night for him so he headed to the lobby to fix a cup of coffee. "You've got to be kidding me." He said discovering no coffee had been brewed. Kim lifted her head up finally noticing Charles' broad figure. "Is there something wrong?" She asked sincerely. Charles sighed and shook his head. When he met Kim's hazel eyes he wanted to dive right over the desk and relieve his stress. She saw Charles had a coffee cup in his hand yet, there wasn't any coffee. She smiled after connecting the dots. "I can make some coffee." Before Charles could refuse, Kim got up to prepare a fresh pot. As she reached up to retrieve the Folgers from the wooden cabinet, Charles caught a whiff of perfume, Bath and Body Work's moonlight path. He knew because he'd recently bought a set of it for his older sister. Charles stood there studying Kim's every move. He watched her purple polished nails struggle with opening the lid to the coffee container. He breathed in as she went from container to the coffee maker and was taken away when she spoke to him. *Say something idiot!* He fell from his fantasy. "I apologize. What did you say?" Kim chuckled. "I said, 'got a long night tonight'?" Charles rubbed his neck attempting to ignore the pain in her presence. "Mhmm" Was all he could say that would make sense. They stared at each other until it was awkward then quickly looked away. "How was your day?" Charles asked. Kim met his green eyes once more letting a yawn slip out. "Excuse me," she smiled. "Well, I guess that answers it." They laughed. "As usual, it was busy…. Well the morning was. The evenings are a bit slow." Charles nodded. "I appreciate what you do around here." That was the truth. Kim's peanut butter toned cheeks blushed and she couldn't hide back her crest smile. "Thank you." They stood staring at each other again. Kim rested her left hand on the counter answering the question Charles was curious about; No, she was not married. Kim followed his eyes thinking they'd been fixed on the coffee maker and she soon remembered her reason for getting up in the first place. "Seems as if it's done." She inhaled the scent. "I think I might get some too." Although she was leaving in an hour, she had the desire to stay longer. After fixing their cups of coffee and talking about how they like their coffee, Charles had recognized he spent most of his time socializing with Kim. "Kim, I do apologize for taking up some of your time." "No, don't its fine." Kim interjected. "The most attention I get is whenever the phone rings, and half the time it's not even for me." She joked. Charles loved her sense of humor and he wanted to spend more time with her, outside of the job. "I know this may not be appropriate, but I really enjoyed talking to you and…." She cut him off again her right hand held up. "Charles, let me stop you right there." Charles hung his head full of jet black curls down in embarrassment. Kim sighed wishing their conversation had not gotten to this point. "Not that I don't think you're a good guy it's." She paused unable to carry on. "You have a boyfriend." Charles waited for the confirmation. "No… that's not the reason." She looked to her right at her desk and the idea came to her. *Oh Kim let `em know.* She quickly walked over to her desk and grabbed the yellow painted picture frame. When she stood in front of Charles she flipped it over revealing a picture of two kids, a boy and girl, with big kool- aid smiles hugging her. "You have kids?" Charles laughed relieved. "Twins" She said confirming his statement. "So?" Charles said blankly. This time Kim held back her excitement. "You don't mind?" She was confused. Charles thought to himself *if she only knew… maybe some other time.* He would tell her about his son when he was ready plus there was more to that story. "Nah, I like kids. I'm an uncle and my niece is loved as if she were my own." To hear him say that warmed Kim's heart. "So you were going to ask?" She referred back to the previous question. "Yes." He took his second chance. "Would you like to have dinner this weekend?" "Wow, so soon?" Kim joked. "Hey!

It can be whenever you want." Charles laughed. "Saturday is fine." She said hopping her mother would be willing to watch Kimora and Kimar. "Great I'll pick you up at 7." Kim nodded and wrote down her information on a "while you were out" message sheet and handed it to Charles who was happier than a person who had won the lottery.

Chapter 5

Mya checked her watched. *Where is this bus?* She thought. It was five minutes late. Usually this wouldn't bother her except this time she was headed to the post office and she had to be there before they closed at 5:00. It was 4:30. She checked the bus app that tracks the location and arrival time of the Saluki Express. Mall bus arrives in 2 mins, it read. Mya calmed herself and waited patiently.

She sat in her seat gazing out the window like she enjoyed doing every time she was on the road. The bus came to a break at the Amtrak train station and she thought about the time Antonio came to visit her. She hoped he was going to appreciate the clothes she bought him and she prayed they all fit him. He'd been working out lately and she didn't know how successful he'd been since their last encounter.

As soon as she pulled number 55 from the machine she regretted it remembering she had so many things to send and did not have them packaged. Luckily she found a red box, Antonio's favorite color, to put the items in. She packed a few spring shirts she'd like to see him in along with a couple of sweaters, wife beaters, and a black adidas work out shirt; size XL. She slid the card in the box, sealed it up, paid for the postage, and was out the door. Antonio should receive his present in two days.

"The weekend took forever to get here." Mya groaned to Riley sitting in the bus seat on her right. "I'm telling. This week was hectic. I had two exams and a presentation." She covered her face with her palm. Mya tapped her shoulder consoling her. "I bet you did great." Riley smiled. "I'm over it! Today is about spending money, so we can have something to complain about next week." "I agree!" They laughed. Mya pulled the wire claiming the next stop; University Mall. This mall didn't have much but one thing it did have were sales and clearance racks, which was just enough to catch the eyes of the two college students entering the mall. "Where shall we go first?" Riley asked. "You said you wanted crop tops. I know Rue21 has some." Riley agreed and they headed West.

Charles was so nervous about today. Though he had hours to prepare for his date with Kim later that night he couldn't keep his anxiety under control. It was three in the afternoon. He'd gotten up early to clean his apartment. His next task was to have his car washed inside and out. He washed his face and brushed his teeth after eating a BLT sandwich. Then, he walked out the door wearing a black Nike shirt and grey basketball shorts.

"Nigga, I'm finna beat yo ass." Antonio said holding a PlayStation controller. He and Luis were playing NBA 2K14; Bulls v.s. Heat. The score was tied 14 to 14 in the first quarter. "Man you ain't gone win Tony." Antonio's cellphone rang; he would have ignored it until he saw the number that resembled a jail line. "Pause it, Louie! Pause it!" He commanded. Luis huffed then hit the start button to pause the game. "Hello?" Antonio answered worried. The operator said the retired 'will you accept the charges?' speech. After he confirmed, she connected the call. "Wassup bro." The familiar voice said. Antonio grew frustrated. "Tobias? What the fuck happened now?" Tobias was known for his misbehavior. Antonio couldn't understand why his brother could not stay out of trouble. "Antonio don't give me that shit, I got enough of it from Dad." Antonio was glad he talked to their father already because he did not want to be the bearer of bad news. "Is that Tobias?" Luis asked eyes full of excited. "Let me talk to him. Give me the phone." Luis reached for the phone and Antonio moved away from him. "Give me a minute." He whispered with his left index finger held. "Okay, you talked to Dad; now what, Tobias?" "Shit" Tobias took in a breath holding the payphone between his ear and shoulder. "Dad told me to call you. Guess he thought you would try to preach that bullshit." Tobias chuckled. "What's the point?" Antonio sucked his teeth. "Exactly, what I told him." "I mean it's obvious now you don't give a damn about your education considering you're about to graduate in two months." Antonio cut him off guard. "You definitely don't give a damn about Luis knowing good in well that when I was off at school he looked up to you and still does to this day. Nope none of that family shit matters because you're so fucking selfish all you care about is money and hoes! Look where both land you every time." Antonio laughed unintentionally. Tobias was silent. Antonio's words hit him; but then again he was fed up with every one telling him how to live his teenage life. "Damn man that's how you feel?" He shot. "Take care of yourself bro. Hey, Luis wants to talk to you. Don't hang up." Unable to reach out to his brother like he wanted to, he passed the phone to Luis who was patiently waiting. "Hey Tobias." Luis was all smiles. Antonio walked out the room hoping Luis didn't see the tears falling from his eyes.

"Man I'm exhausted." Riley said. The girls had been in the mall for two hours. Now, they were enjoying dinner at Taco Bell until the bus arrived. "I can't wait to wear our skirts! Let's wear them Tuesday." Mya was excited. Riley sunk in her chair, "It's supposed to rain Tuesday." Mya huffed. "Dang, it is April. April showers bring May flowers." She sang. "Yup" Riley agreed. "And this is Carbondale, so you never know what to expect." They laughed. "True that." They both ate their loaded grillers and potato sides. Mya washed hers down with an ice water. "Mocha, let's get ready, the bus will be here in 5 minutes." They gathered their things then headed to the bus stop.

Chapter 6

Kim held the phone in her hand pressing the display button on and off. She contemplated on calling Charles to cancel their date tonight because she couldn't find anyone to watch the twins. She pressed the button to show the lock screen, a picture of Kimora the day she lost her first tooth, the time was 6:30pm. If Charles was different than her child's father, he'd be at her place any minute now. Kim was restless as she sat on the black couch in her African themed living room. The pre-downloaded tune on her phone rang and Charles' name and number ran across the screen. It took her a moment to answer and to say hello. He spoke first. "Good Evening." He charmed. "I hope you're ready for tonight." There was much in store for them. "Actually," Kim said dryly. She took a deep breath. "I… My mother … I can't go Charles… tonight isn't good for me after all." She finally decided to say. Charles wasn't going to let her off the hook that easy. "What's wrong? Is there a way I can help?" Kim heard Kimar yelling at Kimora and knew in due time they'd both come arguing to her so she could settle the dispute. "It's the twins; I couldn't find anyone to babysit." Charles was alleviated. He thought Kim changed her mind. "Bring them along." He invited. "No, Charles, I can't." "I don't mind Kim, honest. I'd love to meet them and they'll have lots of fun and so will you." He smiled praying she wouldn't think otherwise. "Mooommy!" Kimar shouted from the room, and Kimora came running to her. Charles heard the sweetest angelic voice through the receiver. It was Kimora explaining her case before Kimar could tell what actually happened. "Honey, go apologize to your brother and put away the toys. We're about to leave." She kindly said to her. Kimora did as she was told. Charles smiled and thanked God. "Give me 20 minutes to get them ready." She said and caught a glance of herself in the mirror hanging from the brown wall. "And for me too." She ran her fingers through her Halle Berry cut. "That's fine. I'm glad you changed your mind." He laughed. "Should I come by 7:30 instead?" "Yes, I…" She corrected. "We should be ready by then." "Great!" Kim disconnected the call then went to check on Kimora and Kimar's performance. "Mommy is so proud of you. The room looks wonderful." She picked out a purple dress with Esmeralda, Kimora's favorite Disney character, and a green shirt and camouflage pants for Kimar. The twins dressed themselves while their mother tore up her closet for something to wear.

Charles checked the address for the third time. *Go up there already.* He hesitated before knocking then checked the time realizing he was already 2 minutes behind schedule. He had to cancel the previous dinner reservations so really there was no need to rush anymore. He pounded the maroon door that had 120 in white nailed to it.

Kim grabbed the twins by their hands that together fit in her palm. "Listen to mommy please." Kimar smiled. "You look pretty mommy." "Yeah, like a princess." Kimora added. Kim's heart melted hearing her biggest fans compliment her. She kissed their hands. "Thank you. Now pay attention buddies." They were all ears. "I want you to be on your best behavior, be nice to Mr. Charles, and when I tell you to do something, do it! Don't ask me why and don't disobey because I will remember." She was solemn yet affirmative. The repetitious knock at the door reminded her that Charles was still outside. "Do you understand?"

"Yes." They chimed in unison. "Be nice to each other too." "Okay mommy. Let Mr. Man in." Kimora whinned. She was eager to meet this mysterious man that had her mother looking better than the stars on the red carpet. Kimar laughed. Kim walked to the door with the twins following behind her.

Charles was speechless and caught his mouth from dropping when Kim revealed her date look. Her short hair was slick back in a wrapped style. She wore green beaded earrings that dangled to match the green and white silk blouse and black blazer. Her high waist black bottoms hugged her hourglass figure. Surely, Charles had seen her at her best around the office plenty of days. Except tonight, she was that star that shinned in the darkness. The scent of Moonlight Path ran under Charles' nose and he smiled to acknowledge her. "Hello, you look amazing." He kept his eyes on hers. "That's what we told her." Kimora said poking her head out from behind her mother's figure. Kim felt a bit embarrassed, yet she covered it with a grin. Charles was astonished to meet the face from the picture frame. She was a lot bigger now and the spitting image of her mother. She met his brown eyes with her hazel. "Hello, Mr. Man." Kimora said unable to remember his name. "Mommy, let him in." She nudged her mother over to the side making her shove Kimar over landing him on his bottom. "aahhh!" he screamed. Kim shot a what-did-I- say look at Kimora and helped Kimar back to his feet. "Please, come in." Charles entered the apartment and fell in love with what he saw. "Mr. Man." Kimora caught his attention. "Are you taking mommy out on a date?" She swung her mother's left hand back and forth. "Yes I am." "Can we come too?" She asked eyes wide. "Of course you can." "Mr. Man do you like my dress?" she flashed a snagatooth smile. "Yes I do. It is very pretty... um?" "Kimora!" She shouted her name. "I can spell it too." "K-I-M-O-R-A" She said proudly. "I can spell mines too." Kimar jumped stealing the spotlight. "Mine." Kim corrected. "I can spell mine too." Kimar ignored his mother's comment and rushed the letters out. "K-I-M-A-R." He flashed a smile. "I'm six." Kimora said grabbing the attention back. "Me too." Kimar jumped. "We're twins." They sang in unison. They all laughed. "Did you coach them to do this for me?" Charles joked. "I can barely get them to play well with one another. This is purely Kimmy and Kimar." "Mommy Kimar said he's hungry and me too." Kimora whinned. "I guess that's my cue. Let's get out of here." Charles insisted. "YAY." The twins screamed. Kim could not wait to see how this date would turn out. She silently prayed in her mind. *Lord please keep my children on their best behavior and don't let this man be a sheep in wolf's clothing. —Amen.* They made it to the car before the rain came down and Charles drove cautiously to Cemenos Pizza restaurant in Joliet. Charles, Kim, Kimora and Kimar sat in a booth, the twin's choice. Kimar kept bumping elbows with Kimora and she kept complaining about it because she was afraid of spilling something on her new dress. After nagging her mother to make Kimar stop, Kim decided to let them play in the gaming area. There weren't that many people at the restaurant most likely because of the weather. The rain was steady coming down and every so often, thunder would roar alerting the customers it had not let up. Kim watched her children enjoy the games; glad her prayers were heard. They'd been on their best behavior. They weren't like Bay Bay's kids though she knew at their age they could get out of line. They were still learning the fundamentals of discipline. Charles noticed the glow in her eyes as Kim observed her gifts from heaven. He held back the tears missing his 4 year old son, Malcom.

The ride back home seemed quicker than the ride to the restaurant. Charles checked the review mirror and saw Kimora and Kimar were buckled in the backseat sound asleep. He laughed. "What?" Kim turned to face Charles. She enjoyed her time with him. "Shhh." He directed her attention to the twins. Kim's heart melted seeing them that way. Kimora's head in two fluffy ponytails was on Kimar's right shoulder, his head full of dark brown curls rested on top of her head. Kim turned down the radio to avoid waking them up. They were going to church tomorrow and she knew how hard it was getting them out of bed on a Sunday morning.

Charles gently laid Kimar in his bed decorated in ninja turtles and Kim laid Kimora in her purple bed with frogs on the comforter. The day they both chose characters with a similar color scheme made Kim jump for joy, and she could not wait to decorate their room. On Kimar's side of the room posters of the ninja turtles and his collection of action figures were on display upon white walls. Kimora had "The Princess and the Frog" movie poster with purple wall stickers. Kim kissed them both and shut the door behind her.

"I really hope you enjoyed yourself." Charles mentioned. "I did. Thank you, especially for letting the twins tag along." Charles smiled. "They're adorable! Kimora reminds me of my niece who's around the same age and Kimar reminds me of my-" He stopped in the middle of his sentence. Kim raised an eyebrow expecting him to continue. "Myself." He lied. "When I was his age of course." He laughed. "Man, my sister Charlene used to beat me up, and then I'd get in trouble if I dare put my hands on her." He could see them now just like Kimora and Kimar. Kim was glad he was sharing such memory with her; it brought a sense of comfort. She invited him to sit down on the sofa. "You have a sister?" "Yes she's three years older and she never lets me forget it." Kim chuckled. "Sounds like Kimora. She was born eight minutes before Kimar; not that it ever made a difference to me.

It means the world to her. I'm surprised she didn't mention it when she met you." They laughed in sync. Charles took a look around the room. "I love this living room. Did you decorate it?" "Yes," She said modestly. "Wow! You got some talent. You need to be on HGTV." He was serious. "That was the dream. I got my Bachelor's in marketing and design and a minor in interior design." "Was?" Charles repeated. Kim sighed and nodded her head. "Thought when I was this age I would be designing expensive hotels, apartment displays, hell a few celebrity homes. Then…" She cut off her conversation and hung her head. Charles lifted it up with his left index finger. Looking into her hazel eyes that shined like diamonds he spoke. "A dream is a wish your heart makes," he took her hand and placed it on her heart. "You feel that?" She closed her eyes to concentrate then once she felt her pulse, she nodded. "Your heart still beating, your dream is still alive. Keep chasing it." Kim wanted to shed tears at that moment. Those were the most encouraging words she'd heard in years. Before she was able to open her eyes Charles pecked her naked lips and she grabbed him closer. They shared that magical moment for what seemed like hours before pulling back. Charles could not believe how big his heart grew for her and she could not believe this wasn't a dream itself. Ignoring the fact she had church the next morning she invited Charles to spend the night with her. *Lord, please forgive me, but it's been a while.* She prayed she wasn't in vain with her choice. Unfortunately, Charles denied her request. He didn't want things to move to fast with him and Kim; especially since she had kids. He knew how things got messy with them involved in relationships. He also learned from his ex-wife that relationships don't always work out and that God is the one in control of the lives of man.

Kim was hurt and her confidence was a bit shattered after he let her down sincerely. He promised her he'd loved to see her again and wanted to keep in touch outside of work. "Before, we do any of this." He added. "I want to run some things by Antonio." Kim was baffled; what did he have to do with their relationship? Is what she needed to know; so she asked, "What does Antonio have to do with our relationship?" with an attitude. Now Charles was perplexed. Where was this attitude coming from? "I have to make sure that our relationship is appropriate for the job. I mean we are colleagues Kim." *I know he is not patronizing me like I'm Kimora.* "I know exactly what we are, maybe that's why this was a bad idea." She threw her hands in the air. "Woah" Charles placed his hand on her thigh to calm her down. "Let's not jump to that. We just had our first date Kim." He held both hand in his and smiled, falling in love with her natural glowing skin. "Listen, Antonio is my boss. There was a meeting Tuesday about some sexual harassment complaints regarding you." Kim let her guard down and paid attention. "I didn't file any complaints... not yet." She admitted. "Regardless if you did or didn't, he heard the comments that Mike and Jacob had said." He recalled sitting in the conference room that day unable to defend her. He brushed the memory and continued. "I want to make sure he knows that I'm genuinely infatuated with you." He admitted. Kim cracked a smile. His comment sent her heart racing a thousand miles a minute. If he wasn't holding her hands she would have floated to the moon when he kissed her on the cheek. "In that case, I think we should tell him together. Plus, I would like to talk to him about the Mongol and Jackal." She twisted her face thinking of Mike and Jacob. Charles laughed. "Good one!" He cheered. "Are you sure you want to do that?" "Yes, Charles. I am. I'm sick and tired of those comments. That's not what my job is. If they wanna disrespect a woman they need to go to a strip club where they don't mind earning money that way." *Man she is on a roll.* Charles thought and was turned on by her strong mind. "Fine. Monday we'll talk to Antonio. Then, I'll let you handle your business." He kissed her again then stood up to leave. She followed him to the door. They shared a warm embrace and another mesmerizing kiss. This time Kim got a hold of his silk based curls and had to remind herself that Kimora and Kimar were in the other room. *Oh God thank you for taking your time with this one.* She thought about Charles. He pulled back and stared at her hazel almond shaped eyes again. "Could you do me a favor?" *Here we go. Go ahead and say something stupid so I can kick you out and regret this entire night.* "What?" she waited for the request, "When you bring up the complaint, don't tell Antonio I told you." Kim rolled her eyes seductively and placed a peck on his lips. "Your secret is safe with me." "Good. Oh! And could you do one more thing?" He begged like a boy. She huffed. "Yes Charles?" He kissed her like the first time then pulled away with her eyes still closed and said, "Have a great night." By the time she opened her eyes he was in his car. Kim placed her right hand on her chest, then pinched her left forearm, and laughed. This was definitely no dream.

Charles drove off in his grey 2013 equinox, once again feeling like millionaire.

Chapter 7

It was Monday morning. Kim kissed Kimar on the cheek and waved goodbye to him as he sat on the yellow school bus. She quickly ran to her 2010 blue Impala to drive to work.

Mya sat at the front desk in the Foreign Language department, eating a banana. "Buenos Dias senorita" A former Spanish Professor of hers said. She was an elderly woman a bit shorter than Mya who was 5'6". Mya smiled at her and chimmed "Buenos Dias. Cómo estás" she asked. They carried on a conversation in Spanish. "Podrías hacerme tres copias por favor?" *Could you make me three copies please?* She handed her the page for Mya to run through the copier. "Por supuesto" *of course.* She got right to the request. Soon after work Mya gathered her things and headed to her first class of the day. Spanish 320a: Spanish Grammar. She enjoyed the instructor and the idea of the class, yet sometimes she thought it was a waste of her time because most of it was spent on other topics other than Spanish. Nevertheless, she attended class every day and on time. Before she knew it, she was in her last class of the day. Spanish 306: Spanish readings and analysis. This class was a bit difficult for her. The instructor was from Uruguay and spoke in the strongest Spanish accent she'd ever heard. This made it hard for her to understand some points. Luckily she shared the class with a familiar friend she often studied with. Today the professor read "El pacto con el Diablo" by Juan Jose Arreola. This short story was about a man who goes to the theater to watch a movie about a man selling his soul to the devil for riches. He finds himself discovering the person he sat next to in the theater is the devil himself and before making a pact with the devil, he runs away. In the end the events that occurred to the main character were all a dream. Mya laughed at the irony. She was content because today it was easy for her to understand this story. Ironically, the main character's name was Antonio. *Maybe he's not sent from above after all. Lord are you trying to tell me something?* She joked. The class ended at 2:50pm. She walked home with her friend Ana like always. They spoke in as much Spanish as they could on the way. "Qué pensaste tú del examen?" Ana asked. *What did you think about the exam?* "El fue más fácil que la primera vez" Mya said *It was much easier than the first time.* "Estoy de acuerdo" *I agree.* Mya made it home before Ana did. "Bueno… hasta miércoles." *Well, see you Wednesday.* Ana waved and smiled. Mya walked up the steps then checked the mail, happy to see there weren't any bills. She entered her apartment and headed straight for her bed. She was exhausted. "Love is not just a verb it's you looking for it maybe call me crazy we can both be insane. A fatal attraction is common and what we have common is pain." Mya heard the words in her sleep and instantly grabbed her phone. "Hey baby." She said trying her hardest to sound awake. "Were you asleep?" He asked. "Yeah, today was a long day for me. I'm awake now." She repositioned her body and sat up to find her headphones. "How you doing?" She asked placing the headphone in one ear. Antonio sighed and was silent. "Antonio?" Mya called. "Yeah?" he replied sounding discouraged. She could hear it in his voice. "What's wrong?" Mya was worried. "My little brother is in jail." "Tobias" She said rhetorically. "Naw Mya, Luis. Of course, Tobias." He sucked his teeth. "I wasn't asking Antonio. It just came out that way." She tried not to grow frustrated understanding he was acting upon his hurt and anger. "I need a vacation." He rubbed his face. "Come here." She offered. "Mya, that's not a fucking vacation! Plus you know I can't take off of work damn. Why you acting so stupid?" He yelled. *Ouch* Mya bit her tongue. Though Antonio's behavior was uncalled for and any other time she would've checked him, she chose not to due to the circumstances. "Antonio I know you're upset right now. I don't mind you taking your anger out on me, but know I'm only trying to help." She soothed him. "Good try, but it's not helping at all. In fact it's pissing me off even more. And where the hell were you when I called you earlier?" Mya was appalled. *Lord please give me strength.* She took a deep breath in. "Possibly in class. I don't know depends. When did you call?" "You wasn't in class at 8pm on a Thursday Mya. I'm not stupid." *No, but you are tripping right now.* "No but you are trippin' right now." She said out loud enough was enough; Antonio was crossing the line by accusing her of lying, something she wouldn't dare fix herself to do to him. "Whatever." He said. "Antonio, what do you want me to do?" "Obviously there's nothing you can do." He said then thought. "Actually, there is. Give me some space. Quit crying all the time about me not calling, and then when I do you don't pick up. Stop trying to fix shit you don't have control over. Let me live my life!" All of this was new to Mya and her heart was broken yet, she fought back the tears. "If that's what you need baby." She waited for his response. He could tell she was hurting and he felt like the biggest jerk on the planet. "Mya I'm—I'm sorry but yes, that's what I need right now. Listen to me. I'm angry at you for absolutely no reason at all. This is exactly why I'm asking for some time to myself. Just let me get my thoughts together." Mya heard it all before and was upset that she took another ride on the emotional rollercoaster. "Whatever you need baby." She could feel the tears slipping. "I love you." He tried his best to encourage her. "Relax, I'm not going anywhere. I promise." "I love you." She said and disconnected the call. Tears stormed down her face matching the raindrops on her window.

Antonio sat at his desk rubbing his eyes when there was a knock on the door. "Come in" he barely said loud enough for Charles to hear. "Hey Charles." Antonio greeted. "And Kim." Charles presented Kim who came in behind him. "Can we speak with you for a minute?" "Or two?" Kim added. Charles smiled at her. "Take a seat." Antonio waved them in. They sat next to each other unable to decide who should speak first. Antonio tapped his fingers on the black laminated desk. "Mr. Gabino." Charles spoke. "This weekend Kim and I went on a date." Antonio was taken back from the confession. "We had such a great time that I would like to see her again." Antonio laughed. "So ask her Charles, she's right there." Kim laughed. Charles specified his words. "I will. I wanted to make sure it was appropriate." Antonio smiled and gave Charles more respect. "I understand." He sat back in the black cushioned chair. "I respect that Mr. Williams, as long as there's no office sex, I don't care." Kim smiled. "Thank you Mr. Gabino." She said eyes brightened. "Yes, thanks!" Charles added. "Is there anything else?" Antonio asked. Kim nodded her head. "I would like to speak with you, alone." Charles took the gesture and stood to his feet. Kim admired his broad shoulders in his grey button down and green tie. Before he walked out Antonio caught his attention. "Williams. How is the scheduling coming?" "Almost done." Charles responded. "Almost?" "They'll be on your desk by today." He restated. Antonio raised an "OK" sign with his right hand and Charles shut the door behind him. "What would you like to talk about Kim?" Antonio asked. Kim burst into tears.

"No, NO!" Jacob shouted at Mike in his office. "Are you crazy? Lower your voice idiot. These walls are paper thin." Mike commanded. He lowered his tone, but Charles could still make out some of his speech. "You have to take your time or it won't come out right." Jacob instructed. "What if he wants them before Thursday?" Mike asked. "Just do what I'm telling you. Don't worry about that nigger. The reports will get done." Charles sighed; he wanted to defend Antonio without revealing he'd been ease dropping in on their conversation. "Okay! Jacob, calm down. You're acting like a mad man right now!" Mike yelled. Charles knocked on the door startling the two men. They wondered how long he'd been standing there. Without receiving permission, Charles stuck his curly head in between the door. "Hey guys could you keep it down. Thanks." He shut the door and headed to his office. Mike sneered. "We have to do something about him too." Jacob agreed. "Yeah, he's getting too bold around here." Mike crossed his right leg over his left giving Jacob his full attention. "What do you have in mind?" Jacob rubbed his brown beard leering.

Chapter 8

Mya sunk in her seat taking notes in her 300 level course: Speech Communication Argument and Debate. She was learning how to flow during a debate. "Alright!" The teacher looked at the time there was five minutes left of class. "Make sure you turn in your flow charts before you leave. See you Friday." She smiled and the students passed papers to the front of the class. *Damn, she would ask for them.* Mya barely recorded anything so she tucked the notebook in her blue book bag and walked out of the classroom. She had one more class left of the day. She wasn't feeling good and chose not to go. She walked home hoping everything was alright.

She boiled a teapot of water. The minute steam soared and whistled, Mya removed it from the electric stove then poured water over the lemon honey tea bag in a cheetah print mug. She was at ease in the bed. It wasn't normal to be home before 3:00pm on a Wednesday. She typed a journal entry for her 464 course: non-violent communication, containing the conversation she had with Antonio. She trapped the tears welling up in her eyes. *Be strong Mya.* She reassured. After she emailed the journal entry to Mrs. Marie, Mya pulled out her bible. As always she closed her eyes to seek God. She prayed humbling herself to ask the Lord to lead her in the right direction and for a scripture that will speak to her heart. Her left hand pulled back book after book until it paused on Ecclesiastes three. She read it out loud beginning with verse one. "To everything there is a season, and a time to every purpose under the heaven: A time to be born, and a time to die; a time to plant, and a time to pluck up that which is planted; a time to kill, and a time to heal; a time to break down, and a time to build up; a time to weep and a time to laugh; a time to mourn, and a time to dance; a time to cast away stones, and a time to gather stones together; a time to embrace, and a time to refrain from embracing." *Woah.* Mya was a God-fearing woman blessed to carry the favor of the Lord. He never ceased to amaze her; nor did He cease to reveal the sovereign God He is. Mya continued reading verse six, "A time to get, and a time to lose; a time to keep, and a time to cast away; a time to rend, and a time to sew; a time to keep silence, and a time to speak; a time to love, and a time to hate; a time of war, and a time of peace." Those nine verses melted her heart and warmed her soul just as she prayed. She finished the remaining 14 verses. "At last," She said reading verse 22, "Wherefore I perceive that there is nothing better, than that a man should rejoice in his own; for that is his portion: for who shall bring him to see what shall be after him?" This chapter alone made Mya think. Ecclesiastes, written by Solomon, expressed his troubles with vanity and the power of the Lord. Mya thanked God for such a revelation. It was true now; she spent the majority of her life in vain. Although knowing this made her heart heavy, she believed Christ died for the lives of men and women. How selfish of her to not put God first after everything he has done. She knew there was time to change that. In fact she heard God speaking to her, telling her not to worry about the timing of things because He is in control. She reread verse eleven, "He has made everything beautiful in its time: also He hath set the world in their heart, so that no man can find out the work that God maketh from beginning to the end." She recalled Hebrews 11:1-*Now faith is the substance of things hoped for, the evidence of things not seen.*

God was definitely moving her and opening her heart making it glad. She rejoiced feeling better about her relationship with Antonio. Again she prayed to the Lord, this time asking for forgiveness. She was in tears by the end of her prayer; these were no tears of sorrow this time, these were tears of joy. *God you are so great.*

Mya sat up sipping ice cold water from the glass she held shaking in her hands. After being frighten from a new nightmare, she found it hard to fall back to sleep. This one was far more unlike any other. Instead of being assaulted by a white man, this time she witnessed someone else. A little girl around age six stared at her, eyes full of pain screaming 'help me'. There wasn't anything she could do. Just like the last time, when she tried to enter the door she was struck by a resilient force. Mya cried for the little unknown girl. Then got out of her bed and prayed to God.

Kim's cell phone rang over and over. She groaned in pain as she grew consciousness. She was cold, in excruciating pain, and she was wet. Why was she wet? She tasted a salty flavor in her mouth. When she touched her left hand to her lips, she recalled that the horrific event was not a nightmare. She had been beaten and sexually assaulted by a strange man in the parking lot. Her head felt like an anchor had been dropped on it. Her ears rang like a tornado siren. *The phone! Kim, answer the phone.* She sucked up all the pain she could take and grabbed the phone from the back seat. "Hello." She could barely make out words. Her mother shouted in full fury. "Kimberly Antoinette Johnson! Where the hell are you? I have been calling you and calling you. Did you forget you had kids? Now you know I love my grandbabies but I have a life too! Shit made me miss choir rehearsal." Kim fixed her lips to mumble. "Hello? Kim? What are you saying?" Her mother calmed down feeling uneasy. Her intuition told her to calm down, shut her mouth, and listen. "Help! HELP!" Kim cried. "Her mother dropped the phone causing Kim's father to pick it up. "Kimberly this is your father? Babypoo where are you?" Kim was crying hysterically. "Daddy, please help me." His heart dropped and he'd thought he was having a heart attack getting short of breath. He asked. "Kim where are you?" Kim was falling back into unconsciousness, "KIM!" He shouted and before she fell into the light she said. "Emerson Electricity."

Chapter 9

Antonio sat at his desk reviewing projects all the employees surprisingly turned in on time this week. There was a heavy knock on the door and Antonio granted access. He was stunned to see two officers in uniform flashing their badges at him. "Antonio Gabino?" One asked. "Yes" Antonio confirmed. "Heard you were the manager around here; for the evening shift is it?" The other asked. "Correct" Antonio said confidently. The same officer recorded it on his pad while the other continued. "We'd like to ask you and the rest of the employees here some questions." Antonio agreed and called Kim at the front desk to warn the others. They still had not arrived yet. There was no answer. Antonio was embarrassed and gulped. "Okay officers what would you like to know?" The officers took a seat and began the interrogation. "You're familiar with your front desk worker, Kimberly Johnson, correct?" "Correct." Antonio replied, still confused. "How familiar?" The same officer questioned. "What do you mean?" He asked before he answered. The officer adjusted his seating. "Have you ever been intimate with her?" "No!" Antonio shot quickly. The other officer chimed in.

"Not ever. Even before you received this position?" "No! I met her when I started working here." Antonio was firm. "How long have you been employed at Emerson Electricity?" "about two months." He said exactly. The officer recorded that as well. "You've been here for two months and never made an attempt to get closer to Ms. Johnson?" Antonio couldn't believe they were questioning him like this. "Gentlemen forgive me, what is this all about?" "Answer the question first Mr. Gabino." The officer commanded. "No. I have a fiancé." Yeah, yeah, Mya wasn't his fiancé and he knew lying about it wasn't good for his record but he needed something convincing. "How long have you been engaged?" The officer fixed his dark-brown eyes on him. "A month." Antonio responded. "What's your fiancé's name?" The officer was ready to record. "Mya, Mya Miller"

"Could she confirm where you were on Thursday, April 10th at 4:25 am?" The officer flipped to a new sheet of paper. "Actually, no because she lives out of town" He was cut off by the green eyed officer glaring at him. "You and your girlfriend are long-distance dating?" "Fiancé," Antonio corrected and liked the sound of it. "Yes, she is an undergraduate student at SIUC. We met at that university." The officers recorded his statement. "Where were you on Thursday, April 10th between 11 am and midnight?" The green eyed officer asked. "I was home sleeping." "Where do you live?" The other asked. "Plainfield." "What time did you leave Emerson Electricity?" "Same time I leave every night 10:30pm" "Was there anyone else in the building?" Antonio thought to himself. "Yes. Michael Clark, he's an evening employee. He should be here by now." Antonio checked his gold Michael Kors watch. There was a brief moment of silence. Antonio repeated his question. "Can you tell me what this is about now?" The brown eyed officer whispered to the green eyed officer who snatched a photo from a manila envelope and placed it on the desk. Antonio was disturbed by the photo of a battered Kim and covered his mouth. "Oh my God" he said, "Who did this?" He was full of anger. "That's what we would like to know." The brown eyed officer said. "Mr. Gabino, are you aware of any relationships Kim had?" He considered the day Kim and Charles were in his office. He pushed the picture back to the officers and one placed it back securely in the envelope. Antonio took a sip of water and a deep breath. "I know her and an employee came in my office two weeks ago. They told me they'd gone on a date and wanted to continue seeing each other. I didn't see any harm in it. In fact I thought they looked good together." The brown eyed officer raised his eyebrows. "So you approved of their relationship?" Antonio shrugged his shoulders. "Yeah." The green eyed officer asked, "What's this employee's name?" "Charles Williams." The green eyed officer flipped to a new sheet. "What about the other employees." "Yeah what are their names?" They were both in attention. "Michael Clark and Jacob Polanski," *Where the hell are they?* Antonio wondered.

Charles had been mourning since that morning. Today was his son's birthday who would have been six. Charles replayed the heart shattering day in his mind after having a nightmare about it. His ex-wife had been a crack addict to heal with her post-partum depression of their first and only child. Charles did his best to fix their marriage. Sadly, all the begging God and taking her to church was not enough to change her heart. In order to avoid a divorce he'd moved out and took Malcom with him. One day his wife, Tiffany, showed up at his door step weeping. "Charlie, I need help. I'm tired of living this way." Her bloodshot eyes met his. Feeling his intuition tell him otherwise, he let her in. She sat on the black leather couch closing her jacket as she shivered. "I'd been clean for two weeks now." She grinned. "Are you proud of me?" Charles stood forcing his tears back. "Yeah Tiff." He empathized. "I'm proud of you." Tiffany lay back looking around. "Wow, this place looks beautiful." Her misty grey eyes caught a picture of Malcom and Charles. Tiffany shot up and grabbed the picture. Charles watched as she held it tightly and a tear ran down her pale freckled cheek. "My two babies." She traced the outline of their smiles. She placed the photo back on the shelf and hurried to Charles. "Let's start over Charlie. I'm gonna change I promise." She grabbed his faced and forced a kiss on his lips. Charles melted feeling her wet tongue wrap around his and he picked her up and set her on the dining room table. She threw down her jogging pants. He pulled down his pajamas bottoms. He kissed her neck in between the love making. "I love you." She ran her fingers through his hair. They came together in ecstasy. Charles carried her to the bathroom where they showered together. He rubbed lotion on her ivory skin and dressed her in one of his t-shirts. "I missed you." He kissed her forehead. She giggled feeling like a little school girl. "I can't stay away from you Chew Chew." She called him by his high-school nick name. Chew stood for Charles Hakeem Emmanuel Williams. Ready for round two, Charles pushed her on her back. "Hey," She stopped him in his tracks. "I'm tired." She smiled. "Let me fix my hair." "Oh come on." He begged. She pecked him on the lips and gave him a stern look. "When I come back," she promised. He rolled his eyes and huffed. "Hurry up." He said then slapped her on the butt as she walked to the bathroom. Charles questioned why she walked pass the master bathroom and chose Malcom's instead.

He'd been waiting for what felt like hours for Tiffany to return. Though she was known for spending eternity in the bathroom, Charles' intuition told him to check on her. He knocked on the bathroom door. After hearing no response he slowly opened the door; no Tiffany. He stood in between the doorway and turned his attention down the hall where he heard a soft cry coming from Malcom's room. He headed down the hall. Malcom's door was cracked just enough for Charles to see Tiffany holding Malcom's body resting tightly in her arms. He pushed the door open and both their eyes shot open. There was blood all over the white t-shirt she wore. There was blood all over the power ranger pajamas Malcom wore. Why was there so much blood? "What did you do?" He asked Tiffany whose pupils were dilated. "He's sleeping" She sang on her high. "Our beautiful baby boy is sleeping." She rubbed his jet black curly hair. "Isn't he beautiful?" She said showing Malcom's face and slit throat to Charles. Charles was panic-stricken "What did you do?" Tiffany placed Malcom back in his bed. Blood continued to run on the sheets. "Shhh" She placed her bloody finger to her mouth. "He's sleeping." She walked over to him seductively and yawned. "I'm sleepy too." She threw her body on Charles. He caught her out of instinct. Blood stained his shirt. Tears streamed down his tan skin. She sunk her face in his toned chest and pulled at his shirt bawling. Charles breathed heavily and snatched her away causing her to fall to the ground. She was flabbergasted as she broke her fall. She laughed uncontrollably staggering to her feet. "You fool!" She spat. Charles was terrified; he'd never seen her like this. This could not be Tiffany. "Tiffany" He called "What did you do?" He repeated. "YOU LEFT ME!" She spat, "IN THE FUCKING COLD." She shot her index finger at him. "YOU TOOK MY BABY AWAY FROM ME. I CARRIED THAT THING FOR NINE MONTHS, RUINED MY FIGURE, CAUSED ME SO MUCH PAIN; THAT LITTLE BASTARD!" She contradicted herself. Charles was speechless. "I LOVE YOU! WHY DID YOU LEAVE ME… ALONE? WHY DID YOU TAKE MY BABY? I LOVE YOU." Tiffany was so high she didn't make any sense. "I WAS A GOOD MOTHER." She slurred her words "A GOOD MOTHER!" She said louder. Charles looked at her then back at their lifeless son. "THEN WHY DID YOU KILL HIM?" He shot. She shushed him again and ran to Malcom placing her hands over his ears. "He's sleeping." She rubbed his lips and kissed them gently. "NO" Charles yelled. "He's dead. Look at all this blood Tiffany. You killed him." Tiffany cried. "No, No. I love him. I wouldn't do that. I'm a good mother. I'm a good mother Charles." She returned to him. He slapped her with force. She screamed in pain and grabbed her face. "Why did you do that?" "LOOK AT WHAT YOU DID TIFFANY!" He grabbed Tiffany, showing her to Malcom. Tiffany, finally realizing what she did, hid her face on Charles' chest. "OH MY GOD." She wailed. "I killed my baby." She beat his chest. Charles continued crying while holding Tiffany in his arms. Once she calmed down. He took her to the living room. He kept his eyes on her as she explained everything to the cops. *Why God why?*

"Thank you Mr. Gabino" The green eyed officer stood to his feet. "We'll let you know more once we speak with the other employees." Antonio stood to his feet and extended his right arm. The brown eyed officer shook his hand following the other officer. "Appreciate your cooperation sir. Have a good one!" He said. Antonio led them to Mike's office. He was sitting at a brown desk sipping on fresh brewed coffee when the knock at the door startled him. He damn near spit coffee all over the place when he saw the uniforms of officer Spanks and Luther enter through the door. "Good evening Mr. Clark." He met his brown eyes with Mike's. "My name is Officer Spanks, this is Officer Luther. We would like to ask you a couple of questions." Mike set his mug down and leaned back in his seat. "Certainly, please have a seat." "Sir, are you familiar with a Kimberly Johnson?" "Of course, the front desk worker." He said cheerfully. Officer Luther nodded. "Mr. Clark where were you this morning at 4:25 a.m." They both had their pens resting on the legal pads in their hands. "I was home with my lovely wife." He turned the frame on his desk revealing his wedding photo. "Beautiful woman." Officer Spanks complimented. "How long have you two been married?" "Five years, let me tell you she can be a pain in the as... butt, but I love her to death." He paused at his choice of words. "To death hu?" Officer Luther repeated. Mike laughed. "Are you gentlemen married?" The officers looked at each other. "Sir, I think it's best if we're the only ones asking the questions. This isn't a tea party." Mike looked down at his coffee mug and his cheeks turned rose red. "I understand. Please, ask me anything you need to." The officers asked him the same amount of questions as Antonio. After answering them confidently, the officers thanked him for his time and Mike led them to Jacob's office.

Jacob was on the phone with a customer, she was upset about the extra charges added to her bill. "Ma'am please lower your voice." He ordered. She continued to holler. KNOCK KNOCK. "Ma'am could you please hold?" He requested without waiting for a reply. He got up to open the door. "What do you want?" He fussed at Mike, who directed his eyes to the left initiating there was someone else besides him. "These officers would like to speak with you." Mike presented the officers. Jacob's eyes grew in size. "Richard Spanks! How ya doing pal?" He shook hands with officer Spanks. "I'm alright Jacob. How are you?" Mike was astonished. "You two know each other?" "Sure! Spanks and I were on the same football team back in the day. Spanky Panky." He patted him on the shoulder. "Come on in." "Hey Mike, could you take this call for me." Mike stood confused. "Sure. Transfer it to me."

"Jacob I hope this isn't me being too forward but since I am here on business, I would prefer to stay on the matter at hand." Officer Spanks nodded his head. "I agree" Jacob said. He relaxed in the grey rolling chair. The officers sat in the black cushioned seats in front of Jacob's desk. "Are you aware of what happened to the front desk worker this morning?" Jacob looked concerned, "Who? Kim? Something happened to her?" Officer Luther flashed the same photo he flashed to Antonio and Mike. Jacob wanted to vomit. He shut his eyes quenching in disgust. "She was assaulted in the parking lot of Emerson Electricity." Officer Spanks spoke up, "Jacob, what time did you leave the office last night?" "Last night? At 9:30 pm. In fact, I left out with Antonio. We were discussing reports." "Mr. Gabino didn't mention walking out with you." Officer Luther interrupted. "Maybe because he was irritated, or seemed that way, while we were talking. You see, things have changed around here; since then he's been grouchy." "What do you mean?" Officer Spanks questioned. "Yes, describe this behavior." Luther wanted to know. The men were at attention. Jacob sighed, "He's new to the company and I think he's trying to be the enforcer; you know big man at large. He isn't too focused on building relationships with his employees; it kind of sucks if you ask me, because he doesn't show compassion." He swatted his hand through the air. "Now that were on the topic of relationships, how was your relationship with Kim?" Officer Spanks asked. Jacob laughed. "Nothing much to say, boys. 'Hi and bye', an occasional 'thank you.' Would you consider that as a relationship?" "Never got intimate?" Officer Spanks eye balled him as if he could see the answer written on Jacob's forehead. "Nah. Kim's a beautiful woman. I just couldn't see myself playing for another team; If you catch my drift." "Actually, Jacob I don't" He responded. "Could you explain?" Officer Luther spoke, "Yes, are you implying that you're not attracted to women… or…" Jacob cut him off immediately. "Oh God no! Gentlemen please." He raised both hands in the air. "Black women; I'm not attracted to black women." The officers took note. "Would you happen to know anyone around the office that might be? Preferably to Kim." Jacob hesitated before answering. "There's an employee named Charles, been working here for about six months. He can't keep his eyes off of her." "Charles Williams?" Officer Spanks asked. "Yep that's him. Have you talked to him yet?" "We would like refrain from answering questions Mr. Polanski." Jacob zipped his lips and threw away the key. "So where were you between 11am and midnight?" "At home in my bed." "Can anyone confirm this claim?" "My mother. I live with her. Well actually, she lives with me." He said gaining his pride back. "During the day I'm an in-home care taker. I used to have two clients but since he died, I've been with my mother." "Sorry to hear that." Officer Spanks said remembering Jacob's sweet mother. "She's doing the best she can. I enjoy what I do there and here. Speaking of, I really must get back to work. Are there any more questions?" He folded his hands. "Just one. Could you point us in the direction of Mr. Williams' office?" Jacob grinned and quickly stood to his feet. "Certainly." The officers followed him through the hallway to Charles' office. Without knocking Jacob burst through the door and his mouth dropped. He turned to the officers who both stood puzzled. "Well this is awkward." Jacob checked his watch, it was 8:30. *Where are you Charles?*

Charles couldn't force himself out of bed. He had not eaten all day and only got up to use the restroom and to find tissue. When it finally hit him that he'd missed both jobs without calling off he found the strength to phone Antonio.

Antonio picked up on the first ring. "Antonio Gabino." Charles coughed to clear his voice. "Hello, Antonio." He said in a low tone. "Charles! Where the hell are you?" Antonio was irritated. "I'm at home. Listen Antonio…" "No you listen! The cops are here questioning everybody in the office. Something happened to Kim." Charles' heart dropped. "What happened to

Kim?" He clenched the phone. "She was attacked in the parking lot early this morning. She looked bad man. You're looking bad too since you're at home." "Where is she?" He ignored Antonio's comment. "I don't know; the hospital?" "WHERE?" He shouted almost in tears. "I don't know!" Antonio retorted. Charles threw his head back. "God, why?" He cried. Antonio could hear the sorrow in his voice. He knew Charles cherished the relationship with Kim and he knew how powerful being in love was. It could make a man go crazy. "Charles. I'm sorry I had to tell you this. Is there anything I can do?" Charles sniffed. "If you find out where she is, send her some flowers from me. I won't be in the office for a while. I just can't Antonio... Mr. Gabino. My son died today...not today, today is his birthday. He died two weeks ago." The tears burst from his eyes like a fire hydrant. "Hey! Charles say no more. I will do that for you. You take as much time as you need." Antonio sat on the phone waiting for Charles to calm himself. "Thank you." He cleared his throat. "Thank you Antonio. I appreciate it." "You take care of yourself. Call me if you need something man." Antonio meant it. "Thank you." Charles disconnected the call. *Oh God why?*

The policemen ended up back in Antonio's office. "Did you guys need anything else?" Jacob answered the question for them. "Charles." Officer Spanks glared at Jacob. "Thanks Jay We got it from here." Jacob huffed and returned to his office mumbling something under his breath. "I just got off the phone with him. He's at home." The officers were still puzzled. "His son died two weeks ago and he's in mourning. Plus hearing the news about Kim was hard for him." Antonio said sincerely. "You told him about Kim?" "Yes."

"He didn't know before you called him?"

"No he was in shock."

"Tell us more..."

Charles set the half empty bottle of gin on the mini bar in the dining room of his apartment. He took a sip and curse aloud. "SHIT" He took a large gulp and his throat went numb from the burning sensation. "God! What did I do to deserve this? I was a good husband, a great father." He grabbed the photo of Malcom and him on the entertainment center. "I was a great dad." Tears streaming from his face, he threw the photo on the grey carpet. "I hate you God!" He spat. "Why are you hurting me? I am so good to people. I love, I don't complain, I pray. Why do you allow these things to happen to me?" He took another gulp. He found his cell phone and tried calling Kim for the fifth time; it went to voicemail. Charles stared at the contact photo of Kim while the phone was on her voicemail. "Baby, I'm sorry. I love you Kim. You hear me I LOVE YOU. I should've told you then. I …" Charles was crying hysterically. He regretted the argument he had with Kim more than anything.

"I knew you were too good to be true." She spat and the words cut him deep. "Kim. I just think we're moving too fast." "Well, I'm sorry Charles. I can't help how I feel about you. I love you and I wanted you to know." They were at his place this time after enjoying a romantic dinner by candle light and the best sex they'd experience in a long time. Charles was silent. Kim rolled her eyes and sucked her teeth. "So this is it? This is what you are all about?" "What are you talking about? Why are you doing this right now?" He faced her. "You will not turn this on me like I'm crazy." "I'm not, but I wish you would stop acting like it." Slap was the only thing Kim knew to do after a comment like that. "Fuck you Charles!" Tears tore through her eyes and she covered her face with both hands. Charles was still in shock from Kim's reaction. He reached out to hug her but she pulled away from him. She stood to her feet. "Why did you have to do this to me? After I told you about my ex-husband, you met my children; we made love for God's sake!" She grabbed her coat and purse. "Where are you going?" Charles asked. "HOME" She was glad she listened to her gut and drove herself to his place. "Don't ever talk to me again. We can go back to being *colleagues*." She said and slammed the door behind her.

KNOCK KNOCK KNOCK the door shook. Charles stumbled to it, bottle in his left hand. He slowly opened it and smiled. "Hey officers." He said to the men in uniform. "Mr. Williams?" Charles nodded. "Mr. Williams you're under arrest for the sexual assault of Kimberly Johnson." Charles put the bottle to his mouth and finished till the last drop disappeared. He dropped it, and then held both arms out and said. "Do what you gotta do."

Chapter 10

"Are you serious Mya? He told you that?" Riley said in amazement.
"Yes," Mya took a bite of her boneless wings. It was a Saturday evening
and they were having dinner at Buffalo Wild Wings. "I don't understand
where all this mess came from. I thought the long distance gave us enough
space." She shook her head. "Did you tell him that?" Riley sipped her
sierra mist. Mya responded shaking her head. "I didn't wanna argue, he
was already upset about something. You know, every time he's mad at the
world he takes it out on me? I don't mind that but at least tell me what the
problem is." She rolled her eyes. Riley raised her hand as if she was in
church. "Preach it sista! What's his problem? I need you to tell him not to
be so mean." Mya sucked her teeth. "I love Antonio, but I don't know if I
can put up with this. I'm already worried that he's cheating on me, now he
needs space." Riley almost choked on her drink. "Cheating on you? Mya
what has he done to make you believe that?" Mya was almost in tears. "He's
hasn't done anything. I just." She sighed. "I keep thinking he's going to
repay me for what I did to him." Mya burst into tears. Riley handed her a
tissue. "Mya, that happened months ago. I don't think he would do that.
Plus, didn't he tell you he would act like it never happened?" She smiled at
Mya hoping to boost her confidence. Mya smiled thinking of what Antonio
said. "Yeah, he did but I—". "But nothing" Riley over ruled. "Listen, you
need to calm down. I don't want you thinking bad thoughts for no reason."
Mya appreciated having such a good friend. "Thanks girl. You always know
what to say. What would I do without you?" Riley laughed. "Probably save
some money." They laughed so hard that some of the guest turned to find

out the commotion. "Girl look at them. They probably think we're drunk." Riley said eyeing the curious observers. "Yeah and all these cups on the table ain't too convincing." They hooted. "You know what, dinner is on me tonight." Mya claimed. "Hey! I'll drink to that." Riley raised her glass. "Salud!" Mya yelled. "I don't know what that means, but salud!" Mya giggled and the two enjoyed the rest of their night.

✳✳✳✳✳✳

"Kim...Kimberly." the soft voice sang. "Who's there?" Kim looked out in the distance but all she saw were mountains painted green and streets made of gold. She took a step and was surprised when she noticed her feet were wet. *What's this?* With her head facing downward she splashed her feet in the mysterious white puddle. She laughed with joy and found it strange that she was having so much fun as if she were Kimora. She fell back onto the grass and was in awe when it turned into a large pool of the white substance. She let the waves carry her and she looked up at the bright blue sky. As she exhaled, her eyes fell dimming her sight. The waves grew larger splashing her in the face. When she licked her lips she opened her eyes. "This is milk!" She said out loud. "Kimberly." She heard the voice again. "Hello?" She called out. "Kimberly."

"Where are you? Who are you?" A big puffy cloud came toward her. Her eyes grew wide as she stood back on the green grass. She reached out to touch the silver lining. "Kim" It said to her. She jumped back and laughed unintentionally. She placed her hand on her white garment over her heart, this time she felt her chest was warm. "What is going on? Who are you? Or what are you?" The cloud jumbled with laughter. "TiKi, you don't recognize me?" *TiKi? How does this thing know my nickname?"* There was only one person that called Kim by her nickname. "No, it can't be." She said. "Look with your heart Kim." Kim closed her eyes and focused in on her heart. She felt a warming sensation fill her body and her lungs filled with air. She shot her eyes open and tears fell from them when she saw her older brother standing before her. "KYYYYYYYLE!" She hugged him tight. "I knew you could do it." He laughed. The siblings were in tears. Kim kissed him all over his face. "Hey! Hey! Okay. Now, that's enough." He joked. Kim let go and took another look at him. "What?

I don't understand Kyle what is going on?" He took her left hand. "Kim, look around you?" She faced the new world. "Remember all those stories mom used to tell us, the ones about a perfect world?" Kim nodded. "Those weren't some Disney fairytales." "So it's true?" She glanced back to Kyle dressed in his white garment. He nodded and smiled. "I'm in heaven?" She smiled. "I'M IN HEAVEN!" Kim leaped in jubilee. Kyle laughed. "Not quite." She paused. "What you talkin' bout Kyle?" He sat on a rock. She followed him. "Kim, you won't let go. This is only a passover for you." Kim covered her mouth. "I'm dying?" She bit her bottom lip. "Yes, Kim. You still have a choice. You can stay here and let your flesh rest until the final day of the Lord or you can continue your journey out there." He pointed to left. Kim saw a cloud of grey smoke float upward into the sky. "What's that?" She asked. "Earth." Kyle said his voice melancholy. *What about Kimora and Kimar?* "We all miss you Kyle." Kim covered her face in tears. Kyle soothed her. "It's going to be alright Tiki. You all will see me soon." She calmed down and her almond eyes met his brown eyes. "I'm sorry I was so mean to you that day. I was so jealous that you got that new motorcycle for your birthday because that meant I couldn't get a car for mine." Kyle died on his 18th birthday in a motorcycle accident. Kim was born a year after him. Since she was turning 17 and already having her license, she wished for a red beetle Volkswagen. When Kyle was surprised with a motorcycle Kim envied him and shut herself in her room refusing to speak to anyone. Before Kyle left he told Kim he loved her and placed a cupcake at her door. "I didn't even eat the cupcake. I threw it away I was so mad." She was hysterical. Kyle rubbed her back as she wept on his shoulder. "Kim, I forgive you. It's alright. I'm proud of you for everything you have done. You're such a strong woman, just like momma. I see you working so hard to maintain. They're proud of you too. Don't let all the pain keep you from being proud of yourself. God wants you to know that he has so much in store for you Kimberly." She sighed and was overwhelmed with emotions. "Kyle. I don't know how I can go on. I love the twins but they're such a handful and I can't spend enough time with them since I work so much." She took in a deep breath. "Mom and dad have been doing all they can to help. If I stay they're going to have to raise them. I can't put that much stress on them all over again. I'm sure it was hard enough taking care of you, me, and Kira." Kyle laughed. "Yeah we were some knuckle heads." Kim joined in. "Remember when we snuck out the house to play in the street at midnight. Boy momma was worried sick when she didn't see us in the bed." Kyle burst out laughing. "She got over that real quick! We got our butts whopped." "Ah memories." Kyle added. "We had so much fun together. Momma and daddy always made sure we knew family was important." Kim said. "I remember that one time you got so mad that you couldn't go to the movies with that one dude. What was his name?" "Ugh Travis. Don't remind me." She stuck her tongue out. "Speaking of dudes, what you got going on now? Wassup with Mike?" Kim rolled her eyes. "I'm glad he supports his children financially though, I wish he made time for them. He doesn't even send holiday cards. They haven't seen him in so long, I'm not sure if they'd be able to point him out in a crowd." "Why don't you turn on the t.v. and say, 'Say hi to daddy'?" Kim playfully punched Kyle on the shoulder. "That's not funny!" "Hey you gotta do what you gotta do." "I know except that's not the way I want to do it." Kyle eyed Kim sincerely "You have to tell them one day Tiki." "I will; when the time is right. Plus, I may not have to." She smiled thinking of Charles. "I have a new man in my life that may be step-daddy potential." Kyle laughed. "Miss one next 15 comin'" They laughed together. "Kim you're a beautiful woman and you have two gorgeous children that love you. If you think this man is good for you all then go for it. I just want you to make sure he has his heart right with God so that he can lead you and the twins in the right direction." Kim nodded her head in agreement. It never occurred to her to even ask Charles about his faith yet, she was head over heels for this man as if he was sent from above. "Yeah Kyle you're right. I haven't even asked this man a thing about his past. I just feel so comfortable around him. I find myself praying for him more than I pray for myself. I want this to work Kyle I really do." Kim was almost in tears."

✳✳✳✳✳✳

Charles refused to eat the second meal his mother offered him. Instead, he gazed out the window cursing his life and cursing God. "Charles, would you please eat something." He puffed an aggravated sigh and reconsidered voicing his thoughts to his mother. Upset or not, he knew there wasn't any justice in disrespecting his mother. "Momma, I'm not hungry right now."

He murmured. "I didn't ask if you were hungry Charles. I'm telling you to eat something. It's been a week, you've been starving yourself. You haven't said a full sentence and the expression on your face has been the same since the day I picked you up from jail." She finished wiping the marble counter top, then sat across from Charles who sat in a bar chair for the island. "Talk to me." She was sincere as she rubbed his left hand. "I love you too much to see you in so much pain." A tear formed in her eye. Charles felt a burden rush over him. It was bad enough that he was hurting, now the woman that gave him life was hurting with him. He avoided sharing his pain to prevent spreading it to his mother, yet here he was silent as a mouse and she still felt every inch. Charles turned his attention from his thoughts to her. "On one condition" He said. "Anything" His mother was willing to compromise. "I need a drink." She sighed. "Charles I'm not going to turn you into an alcoholic." Her head shook to confirm her statement. "Mom, you won't I just want a glass of rum. I'll eat then because I have to." His mother eyed him as if he stole something. "Smartass" She hopped out of the seat and waltzed her petite figure to the bar. "On the rocks?" "No, Ma'am" She returned back with two glasses in her hands. "What's this? I thought you didn't want me to be an alchy." He pointed to the other glass. "This ain't for you. Shit I'm gone need a drink too." Charles laughed for the first time. His mother's chestnut eyes lit up and her heart fluttered. *Thank you God, there is hope.* "Now eat something, and tell me when you're ready baby. Momma is all ears."

Charles revealed all his built up emotions, the ones about Tiffany, their divorce, the death of his son, how his new found love, Kim had been sexually assaulted, and the harassment at his job. Sandra, Charles' mother, was shocked to hear of this newfangled news. She thought most of his sorrow was due to the death of his son and his divorce; she knew absolutely nothing about Kim. Never having to deal with any of those situations it was hard for his mother to find the words. She prayed with Charles and they prayed until the both of them were in tears. He was grateful to have a mother so in tune with the Lord because he'd had given up all hope. Nevertheless, after her prayer he felt a sense of peace fall on him. He was still anxious about his life; however he no longer held the pain or the worry. "Our Father sends us lots of trials to build us up. You may think they are breaking you down but He'll never put more on you than you can bear."

She rubbed his back gently. "When you feel as if you can't handle those emotions no longer, you go to Him baby. He wants to help you, He loves you. Don't give up on your faith." Charles felt a soft kiss planted on his cheek that pressed life back into him. He hugged his mother so tight she almost couldn't breathe.

That night she and Charles prayed again. Hi mother stayed by his side until he fell asleep. She went into her room, got down on her knees, and prayed. "Lord, thank you for this day. Thank you for the life you have given me and the strength to go on. Thank you for my children that I love so much; and please, please, please Father, watch over them. Hold their hearts in your hands, show them who you are, show them a new and better way of dealing with life just like you showed me. I love you Father and I bless your will."

She pushed herself up from the king size mattress she slept in alone and got comfortable in the bed. Before she knew it, she was sound asleep.

Monday afternoon Antonio received word that Kim was still in the hospital and had not awakened from her coma. He wondered if Charles' had been notified of the same message. Not wanting to be the bearer of bad news again, he called off work and headed to the florist to fulfill Charles' wishes.

The florist was decorated with all sorts of flowers. Before walking in the shop it never occurred to him there were so many types. "Need help with anything sir?" The florist asked him. He was a chubby black male wearing a green hat that matched his green apron. "Please." Antonio said full of confusion. "Certainly, what are you looking for?" He smiled. "Originally it was flowers, but I see too many. I don't know which ones are good for this occasion." He looked around in awe. The young man giggled and his stomach jiggled. "What's the occasion?" Antonio didn't know how to put it. "Umm." He rubbed his chin; he looked around the store fishing for an answer. "That's it!" He extended his left hand at the 'get well soon' bouquet. The young man walked over to the violets in a brown basket with purple butterflies and a card. "Would you like this one?" He asked Antonio. "Yes, I'll take that one. Do you guys deliver?" "Yes sir, for an additional fee. Is that okay?" Antonio pulled out his wallet. "Yeah, it's gone have to be."

"Will this arrangement be all for you today?" Antonio nodded. "And would you like to add anything to this arrangement?" Antonio shook his head. "Oh! What about the card? Can I add a message?" The young man nodded his head. He pulled out a piece of paper and a pen then, handed it to Antonio. "Write the message as clearly as you can, we'll type it on the card." Antonio didn't have a clue what to write since this was supposed to be for Kim from Charles. He wasn't sure if they'd made it to the 'I love you' stage or if it was more about intimacy. *Eh what the hell.* He wrote 'I love you Kim' and returned it to the guy. "Okay sir, your total will be $61.72." Antonio paid for the flowers to have them sent to the hospital where Kim was. He thanked the worker for his wonderful service and was out.

Chapter 11

Mya sat up in the bed listening to Anita Baker's You Bring Me Joy. She was only twenty one years old but with the influence of her mother and first cousin she couldn't help but drift to the music of their generation. She found it more soothing and genuine verses the music heard today that promoted one night stands and busting nigga's heads in; it drove her crazy! As she sang along to the lyrics she tried her best to finish the ten page paper for her argument and debate class. Her selected topic was: Corporate should not produce rap music that glorified rape. Her goal was to inspire her classmates to pay more attention to the music they're listening to. Hopefully, they'd realize how it was disconnecting them from the issues of the world. She even gave a speech on this topic and received such support on it she thought to elaborate. However, this topic was difficult for her to write about since she was a victim of sexual assault. The facts and statistics on rape made her heart heavy. Every two minutes someone is being sexually assaulted. On average 237,868 victims are 12 or older and 60 percent of rapes go unreported.

A tear slid slowly down her chocolate cheek. She didn't care to wipe it. It was about time she allowed herself to cry. The pain had been built up since her discussion with Antonio. You Are Everything by the Stylistics blasted from the speakers and Mya could no longer type. Antonio was her everything, in a lovers sense. He stuck with her for so many rocky years. Looking back on their timeline there was no other way to explain their reason for staying connected besides the fact they were in love. She had lost so many friends, booty calls, and boyfriends over the years. Yet, there Antonio was even if he wasn't always there with her. Mya pushed the computer away there was no way she could focus. While resting on her back, she felt lonesome, tangled, and distraught. Not wanting to bore anyone with her troubles, she refused calling friends or family members. Instead Mya cut Chrisette Michelle's "If I Had My Way off", closed her eyes, and began to pray.

"Please Father, hear my cry. I am so broken. I am so lost, or I think I am. I know there are some things I don't understand right now. I trust that you are working my troubles out for me Lord. That's why I am seeking you at this moment. I am getting discouraged; I don't believe I can go on. I don't believe I deserve love, your love Father or the love of man. Yes, Father, your love is far more important and I know it does not compare to the way man could love me. I don't want to depend on the love of man. I pray my heart searches for your love Father. I pray that I accept your love Father in every form you give it to me. I pray that Antonio is that form Father because I love him." She paused before continuing. She wanted to make sure she meant every word that came out of her mouth before saying it. The most high worked in mysterious ways and she believed if she asked for something and it was what the Lord felt she needed, it would indeed be given to her. *Father, If Antonio is not fit for my life according to your will, please change my heart.* Her heart dropped and she wondered if her prayer had already gone into effect. One deep breath in and a long exhale was the way she ended this prayer. Once she opened her eyes she remembered her paper was due by 4:30pm. With two hours left on the countdown Mya shifted her focus to that. Though it was still hard for her, she reassured herself that the Lord was her strength and He enabled her to disclose such a sensitive topic.

✳✳✳✳✳✳

"Baby, I missed you." Mya said as a stream of tears cascaded down her face. Antonio embraced her with a tender kiss to her cheek. Her fingertips gipped and traveled around his broad back. With her head tucked in his chest, his arms wrapped around her small waist, Mya didn't want the moment to ever end. She looked up to plant a kiss on his lips. It was an awkward kiss but she brushed it off. They were overly excited, it didn't matter. "I'm so happy you're here. Sit down boo. Get comfortable. Are you hungry? I know you are. What do you want to eat? Hold that thought. Let me get you something to drink. You tell me when I come back. Okay. Stay there, I'm coming back." She laughed. *Where is he going Mya? Shut up and get yo man something to drink.* Another kiss on the lips and she was out. She searched the cabinets to confirm she had enough ingredients to make whatever her honeybee desired.

Mya returned with two red cups of fruit juice. "Antonio, why did you turn the lights off? You know I can't see in the dark!" She fussed. "Antonio!" She shouted after not getting the expected response. Antonio didn't tolerate Mya fussing at him. It wasn't about power or control; it was their way of play. "Antonio!" She called and flicked on the lights. The red cups hit the floor before she did. "No! NOOOO!" She screamed. She kicked but the perpetrator had Mya in the perfect lock. *This can't be happening all over again.* Mya fought as much as her strength would allow. It was no use; the tall, dark skinned guy was already having his way with her. He pulled down her black tights, lifted up her black and white cocktail dress. "I don't want to! Please I don't want to." She begged. "So you don't want it anymore." He said pulling her hand to his penis. She didn't want to touch it. She didn't want him on her. *Where did Antonio go? Oh my GOD please don't let him see me like this.* The look of lust in his dark brown eyes confirmed that her attacker was not going to show any mercy. She turned her head to the side and saw her box of condoms hid under the bed. "Wait! Wait! Could you use a condom?" She prayed he would at least comply with her request. *Oh Lord I hope this isn't giving him consent.* He let one hand free while keeping his body weight on her. Mya thought about taking the box and going up side his head with it, but figured it wouldn't give her enough time to open the door and run. He snatched the condom from her hand and placed it on. Mya closed her eyes and the world went dark.

Mya woke up in a cold sweat thanking God it was only a dream about the night she was raped. Though it didn't happen in that order the attack took place in her room and still haunted her time to time. Mya turned to her right side to see the time on her cellphone. *I should have known.* It was 3:00a.m. It was also Tuesday morning, which meant in three more hours she had to start her day. She moaned, and then returned to her normal sleeping position. "Who in the hell?" She said feeling the vibration of her phone. If it was anyone else she would have ignored it on the other hand oddly it was Antonio.

"Wassup?" Antonio said removing the half smoked blunt from his lips.

It took Mya a moment to answer. *Please don't let this be another dream.* "Antonio? What's wrong?"

Antonio turned down the music playing the background. "Were you asleep?"

Mya huffed. "What you think Antonio? It's 3:00 o'clock in the morning."

Antonio smiled. "That don't mean you was sleep. You could have been up cakin' with yo other man."

Mya couldn't stand when he talked like that. She didn't know if he truly believed she was with someone else. Since he did find her half naked in the bed with another guy the night she was raped.

"Antonio, I hate when you talk like that. But you're right. I wasn't sleep. Well I was. But I had a bad dream and I woke up. Then you called."

Antonio shifted the phone to his right ear. "What was this dream about?"

Mya sat up in the bed. "You don't wanna know."

Antonio laughed. "Maybe you're right. You wanna facetime?" He set the roach in the ash tray.

Mya smiled, "Yeah. I'll call you."

"Okay, I get it. You gotta tell ya other man to leave."

"ANTONIO!"

"Shhh. Girl people sleeping. Damn! I'm just playing. Call me back." He said then hung up the phone.

Mya flicked on the pink desk lamp on her nightstand. She tilted her head just enough to see herself in the mirror. Antonio had seen her plenty of times with a scarf on her head so she wasn't concerned about that. It was the expression on her face and the sweat stains on her shirt that bothered her. After changing into something her body could breathe through and washing her face she called Antonio.

Antonio answered on the first ring. "What took you so long?" Mya cracked a smile. "Chill boo, I had to go to the bathroom." Antonio sucked his teeth playfully. "I got my eye on you." He pointed at her. "Okay Drake!" She laughed. Antonio didn't find it funny. He was ready to talk about the things on his mind. Mya caught his expression and questioned him about his sigh. "Shit been stressful." Mya huffed. "Why didn't you call me sooner?" Antonio cut her off before she could finish. "My trust me. When I'm stressin you don't wanna talk to me." Mya was sick of hearing the same excuse over and over. She was even more upset that he found that as a legitimate reason. "So what are you going to do when we get married and things get too stressful?" Antonio smiled at the thought of marrying Mya and his response. "I won't be doing much talking. You might tho. 'Oh Antonio don't stop'" He mimicked Mya as if she was moaning. She laughed shaking her head. "That's not funny". "Mya you gotta understand it is different now. I'm not with you. Shit. that's stressful enough." Mya looked sad. "Hey. Don't look so sad. You're killin' the vibe." Mya cracked a weak smile. "What are you thinking about?" He set the phone on his pillow. "You, me, you and I." She responded. "I want to be there for you, Antonio. I can't stand that you won't let me." Antonio was puzzled. "Mya it's not that I won't let you, there's not much you can do. I can't hold you or touch you; do the things that would make me feel better. If I see you when I'm already upset, it will frustrate me even more since I can't have you like I want you." Mya was lost for words. "I love you, Antonio" was all her heart could allow. "I love you too, Mya." They blew each other kisses. "Antonio can I be honest with you?" Antonio chuckled "You better be" Mya inhaled, closed her eyes, and then exhaled. "I was worried that you wanted to be with someone else. I don't understand why you want to be with someone like me; especially when there are so many girls out there closer to you. Sometimes I think I'm the reason why you can't be happy because of what happened, because of what I did." She was almost in tears. "I don't want to talk about that Mya. Not yet and not like this. I will say that I need you to relax for real. I'm not going to tell you again. Listen, I wouldn't waste my time; love is not something I play around with. Haven't you noticed, My, how I always come back to you? It's because I can't let go. I don't understand it either. There are things we're not going to understand, like why that night ever happened." Antonio took a moment before continuing. "In a weird way it has brought us closer." He stared down at nothing yet he couldn't meet eyes with her at the moment. The image of discovering Mya with another man flashed in his mind. "You're right." Mya said. "I miss you so much" She blew a kiss. "I'll be there soon." He yawned. "Soon after what? What is soon Antonio?" Antonio rubbed his heavy eyes. "I don't know. I'll get a ticket soon. Can we talk about this later? I'm tired." He yawned again. Mya rolled her eyes. It was just like him to get tired at a moment like this. Although it was now 3:45 a.m. the both of them should have been knocked out. "Alright. You better call me later telling me you coming!" Mya demanded. "I love you" He sang. "Mwah! Love you." Antonio returned the last virtual kiss for the night and hung up.

✱✱✱✱✱✱

"John! John! She's waking up. Our baby is waking up!" Tears of joy fell from the distraught mother's face. His hazel eyes opened from his nap. "Hallelujah!" He shouted. Kim's mother rubbed her left arm keeping away from the IV. Kimora and Kimar jumped from the chair they shared and rushed to their mother. "Mommy!" They sang in unison. Kim's eyes crept open slowly adjusting to the light. It had been a month since she seen the world. "Catherine call the nurse!" Catherine ran to the nurse's station across the hall. Two nurses came immediately. "How long has she been awake?" A dark chocolate nurse with a bob cut and dark brown eyes inquired. "She started opening her eyes about 3 minutes ago." Catherine said with a smile. "Wonderful, let's check her responses." The nurse pulled out Kim's chart from the end of the bed. "I'm going to run a Glasgow coma scale. This is a method to score the level of one's consciousness. I will assess three things: Eye opening, verbal response to a command, and voluntary movements in response to a command. Now don't worry if she doesn't past the first test. That only means she'll have to stay with us for a while longer until her condition gets better or we discover a diagnosis." John and Catherine looked in each other's eyes filled with hope. "Thank you Tasha." Catherine replied. The nurse, Tasha, pulled out a silver tool the size of an ink pen. She clicked the light on and flashed it to Kim's eyes. Kim immediately shut them then crept one eye back open following the right. Tasha smiled and wrote down the number 4 on the score sheet. "Great." Tasha returned the chart to the hanger. "What about the other two test?" John asked curiously. "It's best if we take baby steps. In order to complete the verbal responses she would have to breathe on her own. I don't want to force that until I know for sure she is able." Tasha met eyes with Catherine who looked discouraged. "She opened her eyes though." John cried. "That is correct Mr. Johnson; however, there's a chance she could fall back into her coma. Fortunately, she passed the first test so it seems there's a less chance of that happening." She placed her palms together. "I promise we'll do everything we can to assure your daughter has the best care and will get through this." John grabbed Catherine bringing her closer to him. "Thank you." Tasha smiled. Before completely leaving the room she added. "I'm praying for this family. Don't give up hope." Catherine ran to Tasha and gave her a hug. "Appreciate it dear." Tasha smiled and continued her duties. "Well John, there's some good news today." She rubbed his back. "Yes, there is. Let's pray for more." He kissed her forehead. Catherine walked toward Kimora and Kimar who were staring at their mother in tears. "Why isn't mommy saying anything?" Kimar cried. Catherine guided the twins to the chair she sat in. As she pulled them onto her lap she kissed their foreheads. "Mommy is very tired. We have to let her rest so she can get strong." Kimora wiped her tears. "I thought mommy was already strong." She flashed her wet lashes at Catherine. Catherine sighed seeking John's assistance. He grabbed Kimora and sat with her in the chair next to Catherine. "Kimmy, would you like to pray with Paw-Paw and Nee-Nee?" Kimora smiled. "Yes Paw-Paw." Kimar raised his hand. "I want to pray too Paw-Paw" John smiled "Good, pray with us." Kimar smiled then met eyes with Catherine. "Nee-Nee you have to pray with us." The excitement of the twins brought tears to her eyes. "Okay Kimar. I will." She planted a kiss on his cheek. They all closed their eyes, and then bowed heads. John led them in prayer. Kim prayed in her head as she watched her family praying. She thanked God for a family that put their support in Him. She thanked Him for providing her with children that were as excited about the Lord like she was. It wasn't normal for kids that age to understand the reason for praising God, yet it seemed like the twins second nature. Kimora and Kimar enjoyed praying every chance they got, before eating meals, going to sleep, even driving in the car. She prayed that as they grew their love for praising Him would grow as well. That they would stay on the narrow road and fear the Lord. Kim felt a tear run down her peanut butter cheek. She wanted to get rid of it in case one of them saw it, but she couldn't move a muscle. *Oh God I'm paralyzed* Kim feared her world was about to change for the worst. She closed her eyes and drifted back to sleep with the prayers as her lullaby.

Chapter 12

A week later, Kim held Kimora and Kimar in the bed. After receiving a perfect score on her test, doctors told the family she would be home by the first of June. "Mommy can I water the flowers today?" Kimar argued "NO! Mommy I want to water the flowers." Kim laughed. The twins were always fighting over something everywhere they went. She reminisced about Kyle. "Yes, Kimora you can water the plants since Kimar did it last time." She glared at Kimar. He whined with his head back. Kimora leaped off the bed. "Nee-Nee can you help me?" Catherine rubbed her back. "Of course, Kimmy! Let's go get some water." Kimora smiled. "Can we get a snack too?" Kimar turned his attention to their conversation. "Hey! I want a snack too. Mommy, can I go with Nee-Nee to get a snack PLEEEEASE?" Kimar gave his You-can't-say-no-to-this-face look. "Yes you may." Kim looked at her mother. "Mom, could you bring more ice please and a bottle of orange juice?" Her mother cracked a smile. "Yes my dear. Paw-Paw, are you coming?" John was sitting in a green chair catching up on the news. "No. I'll stay with butter, babe." "Alright. Let's go you two." She gathered the twins together forcing them to hold hands. The three headed to the cafeteria.

Tasha came in greeting John and Kim with a smile. "Good Afternoon you two." They returned a smile. "Kim, how are you feeling?" Kim adjusted her position. "I'm ready to go home, take a shower, and do something with my hair. I can't stand looking like this." They shared a laugh. "Well you sure sound much better. Hopefully by the end of this week you can be out of here." John looked up from the newspaper. "Really?" Kim said. "Yep."

Tasha confirmed. "Now let's check those vitals." Tasha examined Kim's blood pressure, heart rate, temperature, and breathing rate. Kim was tired of going through this process every four hours. After Tasha left, Kim's father set down the newspaper then sat next to Kim. She felt him rub her fingers. Kim wrapped them around his. "Hi daddy" A smile rose on his face. "Hi butter. How are you?" Kim sighed. "I'm nervous daddy." His heart dropped to hear her confession. "Tasha said you could be out of here soon. You gotta think positive." "I know daddy. I'm sure I will recover from this. But I don't think I'll recover from what happened to me that night in the parking lot. Daddy I thought I was going to die and force you and mom to take care of the twins." She started crying. "I thought they were going to lose their mother. I didn't want to leave my babies, or you and ma. I didn't want to have to face reality either. Then Kyle told me everything would be alright." She stared her father in his matching hazel eyes. "Kyle?" His eyes grew wider. Kim smiled. "I talked to him daddy. He was in a place where peace and infinite love dwelled. It was beautiful daddy. We were clothed in white robes; there was a pool of milk, fields painted green. The sky was so blue I don't think I've ever seen it so clear." John caressed her hair slicked back. "Sounds amazing butter. What else did you and Kyle talk about?" Tears kept flowing. Her voice cracked so she cleared her throat before saying, "He said we would see him again. I didn't understand how, but in my heart I believe him." John kissed her forehead. "I believe him too." He refused the tears forming in his eyes. "You talk about things when you're ready Kim. Just focus on healing for now. I love you and I'm always here for you. Your mother and I will do anything for you Kimberly. Don't ever hesitate to come to us. I love the twins as if they were my very own. They are a handle full but your mother and I got the whole parenting down pact. We've raised two beautiful daughters and a handsome god fearing son. We'd do the same for the twins every second we can." He took in a breath. "The first day you opened your eyes, they were so happy to pray with us. It warmed my heart. That day revealed so many wonderful things to me. How much I love you, my wife, and my grandkids. How our Father has taken so much care of this family, and how important he is in our lives. I don't think I would have so much hope if it wasn't for Him." A tear escaped and Kim wiped it from his face. "It was hard losing Kyle." He paused and could no longer hold back. Kim let him take a moment to release his sorrow. He turned his face and Kim grabbed his hand tightly. "Daddy it's okay, you don't have to say anymore." He faced her eyes blood shot red. "No Kimberly its okay. I can finish." He sighed and pulled himself together. "I thought I was going to lose you. But I see I didn't raise a quitter. Thank you for fighting for your life." He kissed her cheek so tender. It was still puffy from the attack and the gauze. "I'm here daddy." They said a prayer together. John shared the news he read in the paper with Kim.

"Mommy, we bought you a balloon!" Kimora ran in with a yellow balloon with the words Get Well Soon written in black on it. "Thank you babies. Come give momma a kiss." The twins rushed to Kim. Catherine tied the Balloon to the end of the bed. "Can you help with the plants Nee-Nee" Kimora asked Catherine. "Yes Kimmy." They walked over to the arrangement of flowers set on the window sill. Kimar frowned. "I wanna help too." Kim interjected. "Kimar you helped last time. Can you bring mommy the orange juice?" Kimar smiled remembering he held the orange juice Kim requested. He ran to her and situated himself on the bed. "Hey! What is this Nee-Nee?" Kimora pulled at a tiny card behind the violets in a brown basket. "It's a card." Catherine was surprised. Most of the flowers were from Kim's parents she didn't remember purchasing this set. "Let me see that Kimmy." Kimora obeyed and gave the white envelope to her grandmother then continued to the plants.

"There isn't a name on it." She walked to Kim. "Here honey. Read it." Kim set down the juice box on the table attached to the hospital bed. Eagerly, she opened the envelope. "Get well soon" She read out loud. She opened the blue card with butterflies on it. "I love you. Charles." Kim covered her mouth with her right hand. "Who is Charles?" John asked stern. Kim smiled. "That's Mr. Man" Kimora said returning from the plants. "Nee-Nee, I have to potty. Can you take me please?" Catherine assisted Kimora to the bathroom, though she wanted to hear more about this mysterious love interest. John laughed at Kimora. "Who is Mr. Man?" He questioned once again. "Mommy's boyfriend." Kimar answered smiling with his front tooth missing. "Kim you didn't tell us you had a new boyfriend." Kim rolled her eyes. "I didn't think it was that serious." John pointed to the card. "Obviously it is. The man sent you flowers and told you he loves you." Kim could not disagree. If anyone in this life time knew true love, it was definitely her parents. They had been married for 30 years. "Guess you're right daddy." She laughed. "So where did you meet this fellow?" Kim cracked half a smile. "We met at work." John rubbed his chin. "That's interesting." He wanted to ask if she thought he was the perpetrator in the parking lot however, he didn't think it was a good time to discuss it since Kimar was in the room. "Mr. Man took mommy on a date and me and Kimora got to go. It was so fun Paw-Paw" He snuck a sip of orange juice. "Oh really?" John smiled. "Did you have fun?" "Yes! I hope mommy marries him one day." Kimar turned to his mother with the juice in his hand. "Mommy can you marry Mr. Man when you leave this place? I want him to be my daddy." John and Kim laughed. Kimar looked at them unable to catch the joke. John grabbed Kimar from the bed and set him in the chair next to him. "Son it doesn't work like that. Mr. Man has to ask your mother to marry him." Kimar looked upset. "Well he needs to hurry up! I want a daddy now!" He yelled. Kim checked him on his vocals; he looked at his grandpa for security. John patted his back, "Kimar you can't rush marriage. In fact you should take it really slow so that you know getting married is something you want to do. You have to share the rest of your life with this person until the day you die." Kimar shot his eyes open. "You mean when Mr. Man ask mommy to marry him, he'll live with us forever?" He flashed a big smile. John nodded his head. "Then one day, you'll ask some beautiful woman to be your wife" He poked Kimar's nose. "Hey don't rush it Paw-Paw I'm only six." Everyone laughed. Kimora and Catherine returned from the bathroom. "Hey what's so funny?" Catherine asked. "Paw-Paw wants me to get married." Catherine looked at John for more information on the subject. John continued giggling. "So who is this Charles?" Catherine inquired. "Mommy's boyfriend." Kimar answered again. "He's going to ask mommy to marry him and he will be my daddy forever!" Catherine laughed. "I want Mr. Man to be my daddy forever too!" Kimora shouted. Kim hushed her and Kimar laughed. "This man sounds pretty important Kimberly. Why haven't you told us about him?" Kim rolled her eyes a second time hoping her mother didn't catch her. "Mom, I didn't think it was that serious." Her mother sat. "He's met Kimora and Kimar I'd say that's pretty serious." She glimmered. Kim smiled. "True, but that was not the plan." "What was the plan?" Her mother shot. Kim smiled and thought there was no way out of this conversation. "I don't know mother. He asked me out on a date, I didn't think bringing the twins along was what he had in mind. Since you and dad were busy and Kira moved to Texas, I didn't know who would watch the twins. When I told him about it, he suggested I'd bring them along. I was skeptical at first but he surprised me and we had a wonderful time, all of us." She couldn't help but smile reminiscing that night. "That sounds wonderful. I can't believe you wanted to keep this from us." She looked at John recalling their first date. John blew her a kiss and she knew he was thinking the same.

Charles dialed the office. Antonio picked up on the first ring. "Emerson Electricity" Charles' voice trembled. "Hello Antonio. Uh Mr. Gabino, this is Charles." Antonio took his seat. "Hello Charles. How are you?" He asked cheerfully. "I'm doing alright. How are you?" "I'm good." Antonio waited for Charles to continue. Charles was hesitant to ask about Kim yet, anxious to know. "Have you heard anything about Kim?" "A little bit. They called and told us what hospital she's in." Charles interrupted. "Did you send the flowers?" Antonio smiled, "Yes!" He searched for the receipt. "They are violets. I even got a card." Charles was relieved to know Antonio was reliable. "Did you include a message?" Antonio laughed. "Yep. It said I love you." Charles was pleased. "Thank you Antonio you don't understand how much you have done. I really appreciate it man." "No problem. I hate to ask, but you know it is my job." Antonio paused. "What's that?" Charles laughed. "When are you coming back to work?" Charles reluctantly replied. "Soon" He sighed. "Could I see Kim first before I return? I need to make sure she is okay." Antonio felt compassion for Charles. From his comment knew he sent the right message to Kim; they really were in love. "Yeah, Charles. That's fine. Make it soon." Antonio gave Charles the address to Kim's stay at the hospital and then they hung up.

Mya just made it home from a presentation. Her entire day consisted of work, school, and planning for the event. Now she was exhausted. All she desired was to come home and lay in Antonio's arms. Most of her dreams she had about him consisted of her walking into the room and finding him waiting in the bed for her. She slowly opened the door expecting to relive those moments. Yet to her surprise Antonio was not there. Displeased, her bag hit the floor, and she plopped on the bed. *Hu, I'm sick and tired of missing you Antonio.* She felt tears spill from her eyes. She wiped them quickly. *No more crying Mya.* As soon as she sat up from the bed, she heard a buzzing sound coming from the cheetah print bag.

Antonio smiled hearing Mya's voice. "Wassup girl?"

Mya exhaled, "I miss you Antonio." He chuckled, "I know. What you doing?"

She fell back on the bed. "Waiting for you to get here." Antonio kept smiling, "I'll be there soon." Mya rolled her eyes. "Antonio you gotta stop telling me that. I don't know what soon is."

"Okay then let's find out." Mya was puzzled. Antonio searched the web for train tickets to Carbondale. "I'll be there June 10th" Mya filled with joy responded, "Stop playing!" Antonio could feel her excited from miles away. "You got someone else coming then?" He joked. Mya sucked her teeth. "What I tell you 'bout playing like that."

"Chill" He switched the phone to his right ear. "Let me get your address." He reached for a pen from his desk. "Okay I'm ready."

Mya gave the address. Antonio recorded it on the receipt.

"Alright My, I gotta go." He waited to hear a groan.

"Alright! I love you." She sang. *Damn, no fight?* Antonio was taken back. "I love you too... Mwah" She returned a kiss and disconnected the call.

Mya connected the phone to its charger, said her prayers, and then turned over to sleep.

Chapter 13

Charles pressed the elevator button that would take him to level 5 of the hospital. His hands were shaking, breathing became heavy, and his mind was circling. He didn't know what to expect once he reached Kim's room. He took each step as if it was his last. Before turning the knob to the door he knocked twice. There was no response. He slowly turned the knob and the door followed. Kim was sleeping peacefully. Charles didn't want to wake her. He sat patiently until she opened her eyes.

Kim reached out realizing this was no dream, Charles was there in her presence. They shared a warm embrace. He gently kissed her lips. There was a scar on her right cheek, he kissed that too. Kim was speechless. Charles held her right hand. To her they were clammy and she knew then that he was nervous. "It's okay Charles. I am alright." She motioned for him to take a seat next to her. Charles continued to hold her hand as he sat. "I have missed you." He spoke finally. Kim shared a smile. "Likewise" He rose to kiss her again. "I have missed kissing you." He said freely. "Me too" Her heart seemed to race a 1000 miles, every moment with Charles felt as if it was the first time. Kim took a deep breath in. It was hard for her to control herself right now. She had many emotions wrapped in one since the attack and seeing Charles brought out the brighter side of things. "I am so happy to see you. How are you?" She asked him. He looked down at the white tiled floor. "I'm here Kim, exactly where I want to be; with you." He kissed her right hand. "Kim, I am so sorry about." Kim pulled her hand back to cut him off. "No Charles. Whatever it is you are going to say. Save it. Let's enjoy this moment." She looked away. Charles felt embarrassed.

"Thank you for the flowers," She broke the silence. Charles smiled. "You liked them?" She faced him. "I love them."

"How are the twins?"

"They are well. They started summer camp to stay busy. I miss them; they have been by my side every chance they got."

"You've got personal cheerleaders." They shared a laugh.

"Yes indeed. They're also stool pigeons." Kim chuckled.

"Why do you say that?" Charles was confused.

"The card you sent with the flowers was a giveaway, but Kimora and Kimar took it further and told my parents you were my boyfriend."

"I have to thank them." Charles joked. "How did your parents take the news?"

"They were surprised at first. I haven't dated since the twin's father. After hearing about our first date, I think they would like to meet you."

"I would love to meet them Kim, when the time is right." He squeezed her hand.

"I love you." She said. "I love you too." Charles met Kim's soft lips. They remained locked as one, making up all the time lost.

Chapter 14

Mya counted down the seconds of Antonio's arrival. He'd been sending her text messages reassuring her that his travel was going as planned. She was elated to finish her last semester as a junior and even more since next semester she would be a senior.

Her roommate Sherry had gone home for the summer, which meant she had the apartment to herself. She spent the entire morning cleaning the apartment. Now she was on her way to go grocery shopping with her friend Sarah.

Sarah drove her white dodge intrigue down West Mill Street. She and Mya talked about their plans for the summer. This would be the last time the good friends would spend together since Sarah was moving to Iceland. "I can't believe you're leaving me." Mya said. "I'm about to cry." She joked. "Awww. You'll have to come visit me" Sarah smiled. "That I will do. As soon as you find a rich man out there, tell him to send me a ticket" They hollered. "What do you and Antonio have planned?" Mya smiled. "I'm down for anything he wants to do. We'd probably spend the entire day blowed." She laughed. "Get so high we don't do a thing but lay in each other's arms." Sarah laughed. "Sounds good to me! Save some money." Mya nodded.

After grocery shopping Mya invited Sarah to her place until Antonio arrived. Since Mya didn't have a car, Sarah was going to pick him up from the Amtrak then take them to Enterprise to rent a car. The girls conversed while watching *Pootie Tang* on Netflix.

When Mya received a phone call from Antonio telling her that he was five minutes way, Mya alerted Sarah and they headed to the station.

Kim was released from the hospital that same day. She called Charles to pick her up so that she could go home. The twins were with their grandparents. As much as Kim wanted to see them, she craved some alone time with Charles. He helped Kim to the steps and into her home. She was glad to see everything had been in its rightful place.

After taking a warm shower, Kim sat across the table from Charles. He made her favorite dish, crab legs and fettuccine. After dinner Charles washed the dishes and cleaned the kitchen. Kim was impressed at his hospitality but wished that she was able to help him instead of feeling helpless. The doctor requested that Kim not handle any task that required her to be on her feet for long periods of time. She could return back to work if she felt it was best. However, being that was where the attack happened, she was going to file for a law suit and resign from her position. The investigation was still going on. The police finally got a warrant for the security camera footage. Kim and Charles hoped they recorded enough to find the perpetrator. Nevertheless, Kim shoved that conversation out the window every time Charles tried to bring it up.

"I'm just not ready Charles." Kim said frustrated. Charles huffed and stroked Kim's hair, now curly after her shower. "You can't shut down Kim. I don't want you to hide the pain." Charles was being persistent. It had been a month since the attack happened and Kim had not spoken to anyone about her assault, not even the cops. "You know the cops are going to come back. You can't fight this until you give your statement." Kim rolled from his chest to separate herself. "I'm going to bed now." Charles followed her and wrapped his arm around her waist. "Kim." He kissed her neck. "I'm not tryna pressure you." She fought off his charm. "Then leave me the hell alone!" Charles kissed her neck again while squeezing her tighter. "Stop Charles, I know what you're trying to do. I'm not falling for it. I don't want to talk about it. I won't talk about it." Charles ran his left hand up her stomach to her breast. He gently played with her nipple. "You don't have to talk about it Kim. I want you to be comfortable." His soft tone and touch was no match for Kim's resistance. "Are you comfortable?" He kissed her cheek. She moaned. He turned her chin to meet her lips. Their tongues danced and Charles continued to explore Kim's body. She turned on her back to face him. He transitioned himself on top of her. They took turns discovering each other's spots. "I want you. Can I have you?" Charles requested. Kim was in utopia but was she ready? Suddenly, tears fell from her eyes. Charles was heart-broken. He kissed her wet cheeks. "It's okay. We don't have to. We can just lay here." Kim shook her head. She exhaled and spoke. "I'm yours." From then Charles knew exactly what to do. He fulfilled his desires along with hers. His lips kissed her wet lashes. He tasted the salty tears. Then he traced her lips with his finger. Kim smiled. Charles fondled her size 36 B cup breast and took one by mouth. Kim felt a sensation of erotic pleasure shoot to her toes. Once pleased, Charles wasted no time traveling to her most precious possession. Kim squealed, ooh, and ahh as Charles rapidly flicked his tongue on her clitoris. His tongue tricks had Kim shouting as if she was rooting for a sports team. On the peak of a climax she grabbed a handful of Charles' silky curls and her juices squirted like a fountain. Charles kissed her quivering inner thighs. She looked at him like she seen a pig fly. "DAMN" She bit her bottom lip. Charles fetched a towel and cleaned Kim appropriately. She still had a hard time catching her breath. They returned to their beginning position. Charles' laid on his back with Kim rested on his shoulder. She was out before he could tell her goodnight.

The next morning Kim felt like a new woman. Charles kissed her upon the forehead. "Good afternoon." Kim's eyes widen. "Afternoon?" She was surprised she slept past 10. "How long have you been up?" She asked Charles. "I woke up at 6 to go for a jog. Then I came back and saw you were still asleep. So I joined you. Since then, I guess I've been up for a while." He chuckled.

"You go jogging?" Kim was impressed. *No wonder he looks so damn good.*

"Yup, I go every morning." He said

She fell into in his chest. "You don't smell sweaty." She joked.

"I took a shower." He laughed. "You definitely could've woke me up for that." They chuckled. "Are you hungry? I was thinking about going out for some food."

"I don't know. I feel a bit tired still." Kim rubbed her head. Charles was concerned. "You got a headache?" Kim shook her head. She lied.

"I'm alright. Could you get me some water?" Charles hopped up from the mattress. "Sure."

When Charles returned he found Kim was no longer in the bed. "Kimberly?" He called. He dropped the green glass from his hand when he heard coughing coming from the bathroom.

"Baby, are you okay?" He turned the nob to the door unable to enter. "Kim unlock the door!" Kim was furiously throwing up. Charles consistently banged and jiggled the handle. When he heard the toilet flush he waited for Kim's exit. She swung the door open. "Don't be knocking on my shit like that Charles. You gone break it!" She spat. Charles was taken back. "Kim are you okay?" His face was pale as if he'd seen a ghost. She wiped her mouth. "Yeah I'm fine." She spoke, her voice hoarse. He hugged her tightly. "I was so worried that I dropped your water." Kim rolled her eyes. "Great now my carpet is going to have water stain." She pushed him off of her and rushed to the stain. Kim found the cup then angrily chunked it at Charles. "I do my best to keep this place clean and here you come fucking shit up. Just like every man in my life." Charles dodged the cup just in time causing it to crash into the lilac color walls. "Kim what is wrong with you?" She rolled her neck. "You are what's wrong with me. If you weren't being such a deadbeat this would have never happened." Charles stood on the opposite side of the bed of Kim. "What are you talking about?" Kim threw a pillow at Charles. "Why are you always playing dumb? Just admit it!" Charles caught the pillow and tossed it back on the bed. "Admit what Kim? I don't understand. Why are you mad right now?" Kim launched another object at Charles aiming for his head. "I'm sick of this Michael. Get out! Get out!"

Charles sped to Kim like lightening. She fought him as he forced her to the bed. She screamed, she kicked, and spat on him. "No please don't hurt me. I'm sorry. I'm sorry. Don't rape me, I have kids. Please don't hurt me." Charles released Kim instantly. She bawled up and cried overwhelmingly. Charles was defeated. He raised his hands to his head, fighting back the tears. To see Kim transition from so many emotions was an eye-opener for him. He knew that if she continued to lash out on him like this then it was time for her to speak to a therapist. She had too much built up in her system and after her assault it would not better her health. Charles sat at the end of the bed bringing Kim's head to his lap. She rested there until the tears ended. Then, fell into a deep sleep.

"Tiki!" Kyle yelled. "What? Why are you screaming?" Kimberly found herself seated in a chair across from her brother. "You can't do this to yourself." He demanded. "Do what Kyle?" Kyle stood to his feet. "HIDE" Kim shot back. "Not you too Kyle, I was hoping you would have some understanding. I'd just been assaulted, and awakened from a coma. I have to figure out how I'm going to get my life back to normal." Kyle beat the desk. "That's the thing! You won't Kim. Life will never be the same from this point on. That's the purpose it's called the past." He lowered his tone. "Kim, this is your calling. I know you don't understand now, but God has ordered your steps. Kim, he chose you. It's time for you to talk about it. It's time for you to free yourself from all the hurt and pain so that He can take those damages and restore them." Kim felt a stream of tears on her cheeks. Kyle rose to wipe them. "Don't turn away from what the Lord has already installed in you Tiki." She released more tears. "I'm not strong enough Kyle." He patted her back. "Yes, you are Tiki. That's why you chose to return." At that moment Kim received a revelation and suddenly grew empowered. "How do I keep this strength? What if it happens again?" She shook in fear. He shushed her and whispered in her hear. "Talk to Him" Kyle kissed her peanut butter cheek. She wrapped her arms around him and felt a warm feeling exalt from his chest.

Kim awoke to Charles singing, "His eye is on the sparrow" silently as she rested on his lap. It was the only gospel song he could remember and the only thing he thought would help. Kim finished the song with Charles. He was impressed, Kim had a beautiful voice; they harmonized well together. Once they finished, she sat up staring at Charles unable to speak a word. "Feel better?" He asked mesmerized in her hazel eyes. "No, I don't" She admitted. "I feel…" She didn't want to continue, yet she found the courage. "I feel ashamed. I feel lost and disconnected. I am afraid. I am in pain. I don't think I can go on, but I want to." Charles was astonished hearing Kim's sacred confession. "Do you want to talk about it?" Kim shook her head. Charles grew angry. "Kim, you lash out on me, calling me some other nigga name, and then fight me off as if I'm an attacker. Then tell me you're not ready to talk about it? I can't understand." Kim grabbed his hand. "I'm sorry baby. I really am." Charles could tell she was on the verge to tears. "Do I want to talk about it? No, I'm not ready to accept the fact that this happened to me. But I am ready to talk about it. Could you promise me one thing?" Charles held her face with the free hand. "Anything." A single tear freed itself. "Promise me that you'll still love me." Charles kissed Kim passionately and they made love like the first time.

"I met my ex-husband in high school." Kim sat on the couch sharing tea with Charles. "They say those are the ones that will last. They also say don't follow them to college, but I did any way. I got pregnant freshmen year. I didn't expect Michael to propose. I thought I would have to drop out and take care of the baby alone; especially once I found out I was having twins." She paused to recover. "We got married that summer. My parents weren't happy, but they didn't want their grandchildren to be born out of wedlock. Things went well until the twins were born. I took a semester off and once the twins were old enough I returned back to school. Only to find out that my husband had not only been sleeping around with a cheerleader, she too had been pregnant." Charles dropped his bottom lip. "I instantly told my mother. I knew if I didn't I probably would've done something stupid. Since I was on a scholarship through the school she told me I couldn't transfer schools. What I did need to do was file for divorce. Can you imagine being only 19 years old filling for divorce?" She shook her head. "I couldn't. It was hard. I did it unwillingly. To this day, I don't know if he was as heartbroken as I. He hasn't spoken to me since then." Charles interrupted. "What about the twins, does he talk to them?" Kim was embarrassed "He doesn't have time. However, he provides for them financially so I don't complain."

"So they have never met their father?" Charles questioned. Kim shook her head. "Damn" Charles said under his breath. "What does he do that causes him to be so busy?" Charles motioned air quotes. Kim hesitated to respond. This was the part she hated revealing about her ex-husband. "He's a professional." Charles stared at her. "A professional what?" He laughed. Kim bit her bottom lip. "Is he a drug dealer?" he guessed. Kim shook her head. "No. He's a professional football player." Charles could not believe it. "You telling me this man is playing for the NFL and can't make time to come see his children?" Charles disagreed. "That's bullshit!" Kim agreed. "I know. I understand he doesn't want to have to deal with you but he shouldn't take it out on the twins." Charles was caught in astonishment. "I agree." Kim added. "While I was in the hospital Kimar admitted he wanted a daddy. It broke my heart that my children think they don't have a father." Charles embraced her. "It will work out. Be patient."

Chapter 15

Antonio sealed the last of three joints. Mya entered the room and the smell of fried chicken filled Antonio's nostrils. "Damn My, you got it smelling good in here!" Mya smiled. "You ready to eat?" she asked. Antonio shook his head and lit the first joint. "You know I like to smoke first." Mya rolled her eyes and headed for the door. Antonio caught her right hand pulling her toward him. "Where you going?" He said handing her the joint. She took it to her lips and inhaled. "This is good." She admitted. "That's Cali for ya!" Antonio smiled. Mya walked out with the joint in her hands. Antonio rushed toward her. "Come back with that." Mya laughed as Antonio chased her around the house. "Mya quit playing before you drop it." He yelled. Mya stopped in her tracks. Antonio wrapped his arms around her 32 inch waist. "Chill. I won't drop it." She took another puff, then passed it back to him. Antonio sat on the couch in the living room while Mya continued to cook. "You sure you can cook while you high?" Antonio joked. Mya laughed recalling a memory of hers. "Yeah I can cook with my hungry ass. Beware though, I cannot bake." Antonio laughed out a cloud of smoke. "That's because you already baked." They laughed in harmony. "I remember one time I tried to make cupcakes. I added way too much water. My eyes were so low I couldn't tell what I was doing." Antonio walked into the kitchen to hand the joint back to Mya. "Well I don't want you burning the house down. Get out of here I'll finish." He nudge her. She finished smoking what was left and sat on the couch. "Go ahead. The only thing left is the chicken." Antonio finished frying the remaining chicken wings until they were golden and crispy. The two shared dinner with one another watching Newlyweeds.

"That was delicious" Antonio kissed Mya on the cheek. "Thanks, I love you." She blushed. "You're welcome." She said. "You ready to smoke some more?" she asked. "Dang you a pothead." Mya playfully hit him. Then got up to place the plates in the dishwasher. Antonio followed to help clean up. After the kitchen was spotless they returned to the bedroom. Mya laid on Antonio's chest. They relaxed in silence absorbing each other's energy. "I am so happy you're here" Mya broke the silence. "Why? So you can smoke all of my weed?" Antonio joked. She turned to face him. "Yeah, that too." She retorted. He chuckled. "I didn't believe you would come." "Why?" Antonio rolled his eyes and passed the blunt to Mya. She shook her head. Antonio returned it to his lips. Mya stared down afraid to admit it, "Antonio I betrayed you. I broke you, shattered all of your hopes and dreams. I was the reason you hated life. I hated myself for that. It was hard for me to forgive myself for hurting you." She fought back the tears. "I thought you were done with me. I thought we were over. Then you come back to me as if nothing ever happened. I couldn't grasp that you, after what took place, would really want to be with me after that." Antonio thought to himself unable to voice any of his opinion out loud. He knew at one point in time Mya would bring up the issue and he wished she'd done it much later in life because he still was not ready to talk about it. Nevertheless, the conversation had made its way to this present so he chose to nip it in the butt. "Mya once I tell you this, I don't ever want to talk about it ever again. Do you understand?" Mya nodded her head and listened anxiously. "I thought about ways to get you back for what you did. I thought about not ever speaking to you again. I thought about ending my life to get over this entire thing." He turned to face her. "But I had a plan, a better plan than any of that. You were in that plan before you betrayed me. Despite everything, I want you to remain in that plan. Even though I told myself countless times I could do it without you, I didn't want to do it without you. It hurt more knowing that I had to cancel you out of my life. So, I gave up and gave in. I don't think you understand me when I tell you I love you. I know I may not say it as often as you need to hear it, but you have to believe me. If me being here now has not proved that to you then, we need to end this right now. I can't have you doubting me Mya. We can't grow if you have doubts." He said sternly. Mya pecked his lips. "I believe you." She said and meant it for the first time. "I'm sorry" She said releasing all the tears that had been lined up. Antonio held her as she wept in his arms. "Don't cry Mya. You gotta be strong. You got to let it go. It's in the past now. I forgave you, and you forgave yourself. You can't let it eat you up like this. I can't stand seeing you all sad, it fucks me up." Mya dried her tears. Antonio kissed her forehead. "You wanna take a shower with me?" She asked. He shook his head. Mya's eyes grew wide. "Why not?" Antonio laughed. "Because you gone get something started that you can't finished." Mya chuckled catching on to what he was talking about. "You don't think it's about time we …" Antonio cut her off. "Nope. You're not ready yet." Mya rolled her eyes. "Fine we won't. Can we just shower together?" "NO" Antonio strictly said. "Mya you may think you'll be able to control yourself, but I can bet you one thing; you can't" Mya rolled off of him. "I bet you I can." She challenged him. Antonio still shook his head. "Give up already. I'm not doing it." Mya rushed out the bed. "FINE! I'll take one by myself then." Antonio shrugged his shoulders. "Good, you stink." He laughed. Mya took off her clothes and wrapped the purple towel around her. She stuck her tongue out as she left her room. Antonio laughed and lit up the last joint.

Mya awoke in Antonio's arms. She nudged him waking him up instantly. "What?" He said eyes still closed. "Get up, you snoring too loud." Antonio wrapped the covers around his face and repositioned himself. Mya grew frustrated and nudged him again. "ANTONIO!" She hollered. He didn't respond. She let out a huff. When she heard him snoring, she got out bed to roll a joint of her own. She couldn't find her lighter so she checked Antonio's pockets for certain she'd find one. It was then when she came across a receipt from a florist shop. Her eyes grew wide when she saw Antonio had purchased a bouquet of flowers and had them delivered with a card that said, 'I love you'. She smacked Antonio out of his sleep. "What the fuck, Mya?" He yelled. "That's what I would like to know." She showed the receipt to him. "What the hell is this?" Antonio wiped his eyes then sat up on the bed. "What is what?" She threw the piece of paper watching it slowly land in front of him. Antonio grabbed it to study it. When he realized what it was he threw on the floor and laid back down. He gritted his teeth trying not to blow up at Mya for her outrageous behavior. "Really Antonio?

You gone ignore me like that?" She hollered. Antonio shot out of the bed. "Mya stop fucking screaming! It's too early, people are still sleeping."

"I don't give a damn about them! You tell me what the hell this is, Antonio." She picked up the receipt "Who the fuck you sending flowers to?"

"Watch your language, Mya."

"Don't tell me to watch shit right now Antonio. ANSWER ME!"

Antonio balled up his fist. He headed for the door to escape what could become a dangerous situation if Mya didn't calm down. She guarded the door preventing him from leaving.

"Tell me." She smashed the paper in his face. Antonio pinned her up against the door.

"I told you to calm down!" He screamed. Mya was in total shock. "Stop Antonio you're hurting me!" She tried to free herself but Antonio gripped tighter. "Are you going to calm down now so we can talk like two adults?" Mya glared at him with fire in her eyes. She nodded her head. Antonio released her and she smack him across his face. He closed his eyes counting to ten in his head. "Tell me who she is."

"Her name is Kim." Antonio responded quickly. Mya's heart sank.

"How long have you known her?" She continue glaring at him. Antonio could see the hurt in her eyes.

"Since I started this new job." He admitted. Mya was crushed. All this time she had a feeling Antonio had been cheating on her. She shook her head in disbelief.

"I knew it!" She launched herself at him aiming to take out all her frustration and hurt on his face. Antonio blocked the blows and finally grabbed her wrist tightly.

"Let me go you cheating piece of shit" She spat.

Antonio spoke calmly, "Baby, listen it's not what you think."

Mya was astonished. "Antonio, you just admitted you've been seeing this girl and you tell me it's not what I think. No, it's exactly what I thought!"

"Mya, I never admitted to that."

"Yeah like you would. LET ME GO!" She continued to free herself.

Antonio gripped tighter as she fought. "LISTEN!" he said shaking her. She breathed heavily. "What, Antonio?" Tears fell from her face. Her heart was broken, she couldn't stand to look at him any longer. "Make it quick." She demanded.

"Alright." He spoke calmly. "I'm going to let you go; but if you try to put your hands on me again like I'm some type of animal, you will get your feelings hurt." He threated. Mya rolled her eyes. "Just let me go!" Antonio respected her command and slowly released her wrist. She stepped away from him still breathing heavily.

Antonio spoke. "There's a secretary at my job, her name is Kim. She is 25 years old with two kids." Mya interrupted "Oh now you wanna be captain save a hoe." Antonio sucked his teeth. "Are you going to listen?" Mya surrendered her hands. Antonio continued. "She was sexually assaulted in the parking lot two months ago. The police accused her boyfriend, a man that works at the office with me. So, he asked me to purchase flowers for her and have them sent to the hospital. I never slept with her."

Mya was perplexed. "I'm supposed to believe that." Antonio stood to his feet, then walked toward Mya. "You better Mya; especially after what I told you last night." Mya crossed arms on her size 32 B cup breast, unable to decide if she believed him or not. He grabbed her by her waist pulling her closer toward him. "Mya don't give me a hard time about this. I don't want to argue." Mya could see the sincerity in his eyes. She wrapped her arms around his neck. They met at each other's lips. Antonio picked Mya up and she wrapped her legs around his waist. Antonio carried her to the bed and threw her on her back. Mya bit her lip and it drove Antonio wild. He forced his shirt off and Mya threw down her silk shorts. *Time for some make up loving* they thought in sync. Just then Antonio's phone rang. Mya sighed as she watched him answer it.

"Antonio!" Charles clutched the phone it his right hand.

"Yes Charles." Antonio said annoyed.

"Sorry if I caught you at a bad time. Are you able to talk?"

"Sure." He said since he'd already answered. Charles spoke as if he had news to share. "What's going on?"

"I just received news about Kim's case."

Antonio's eyes grew wide and he put the phone on speaker for Mya to hear. He placed his left index finger signaling for her to keep quiet. He returned to sit on the bed so that she could hear clearly.

"What did you hear?" Antonio asked. Antonio heard Charles say something to Kim in the background then he continued.

"They identified two men from the security footage." Charles said cheerfully.

"Do you know who it is?" Antonio asked.

"Yes. Could you meet me at the office? I'd rather discuss it with you there." Charles requested.

Antonio looked at Mya. "I'm actually in Carbondale visiting my girlfriend now"

"Oh." Charles said. "Well are you coming back soon? The police need you so they can settle the law suit."

Antonio cocked his head to the side. "Lawsuit!" He said.

"Yes. Antonio you have to come back soon."

Antonio heaved a sigh. "I'll try to be back Monday. How does that sound?"

"Great! Let me know when you touch down." Charles requested.

"Will do. Goodbye," Antonio disconnected the call.

Mya stared at him angrily.

"You believe me now?" He said. She sucked her teeth. "What's the problem now?"

"You weren't supposed to leave until Wednesday!" Mya spat

"Mya you just heard that there's an emergency. I just finished telling you about."

"I don't care Antonio. Let them handle it, this has nothing to do with you."

"Mya it has everything to do with me. I'm the manager of the place."

Mya put her shorts back on then stood to leave. "Where are you going?" Antonio said following behind her. "Out!" she grabbed her black biker jacket. She swung the front door open. "Mya, where are you going without any shoes on?" Mya looked down at her feet. *Well this is embarrassing.* She shut the door slowly and returned to face Antonio. "Babe, talk to me." He caressed her arm. "Why are you mad?" Mya took a seat on the couch. "Antonio, you never have time for me. The chance we get to spend time together, we either argue or you have to go handle something; I'm sick of it." He joined her on the couch. "I understand how you feel." Mya rolled her eyes. *Yeah right.* "You wonder why I doubt you and get angry when you have to leave. Then when I see things that make me think you're actually out there messing around, I get worried."

"Mya, you listened to the guy prove that I wasn't lying."

"I know Antonio, and I believe you." She exhaled. "But what do you expect me to do at a time like this?" Antonio got down on one knee and said. "Marry me?" Mya wanted to pinch herself when she heard the words come from his mouth. "Antonio are you serious?"

"Like the heart attack you almost had" He laughed. "I know this isn't what you had in mind for a proposal." "YES!" she screamed "This is exactly what I had in mind Antonio. You asking me was all I wanted." She kissed him and from that point on, they finished what they started.

Chapter 16

"Ooh Antonio look at this one" Mya's eyes were filled with excitement as they gazed at the dazzling diamond rings. "Mya, we've been looking at rings for hours. Can you just pick one?" Antonio moaned. She hushed him and carried on to a wedding ring set. She tapped her index finger down and shouted, "That one! I want that one!" Antonio was embarrassed as he saw the Kay Jeweler's employee head toward them. "Mya keep your voice down." "Its alright" A caramel skinned woman smiled. "We enjoy seeing happy customers." She presented herself to Mya. "Hi! I'm Leslie." Mya and Leslie shook hands. "I see you found something you like." Mya grinned, "Like? I love it" Leslie chuckled. "Would you like me to pull it out for you?" Mya nodded. Leslie described the ring as she held it close for Mya and Antonio to see. "This is our lab-created sapphire ring. 1/15 cut diamond, with 10 carat white gold band all around." Mya sighed, "Yes. I like white gold. Could I try it on?" Mya slid the ring on, it was a perfect fit. "Antonio look" She flashed the ring on her finger. "This is the one" She said. "Hallelujah!" He sang. "Well take it." He told Leslie. "Great! Congratulations, you two." Mya returned the ring. Then the three headed to the checkout to handle the paper work. "All set. You can pick up the ring on Wednesday." Mya and Antonio were elated. Mya invited a few friends out to celebrate their engagement. They ate at La Fogata, an authentic Mexican restaurant on the strip of College Street. The girls were excited to meet Antonio on such occasion. "I knew it was going to happen. See, Mya, you had nothing to worry about." Mya smiled at Riley, "Fine! You were right." She kissed Antonio on the cheek. "I'm glad you were." The happy people chit chatted about wedding plans and other topics until all plates were empty.

That night Antonio relaxed in Mya's arms. They were resting in on a blanket by SIUC's campus lake watching the stars. "Do you think it's true?" Mya said. "What?" Antonio asked. "That God has our lives all planned out. That He created special pathways so we'd meet our soul mates?" Antonio thought for a minute. "You know what I think?" He turned to face Mya. "What?" She smiled. "I think God put me in the right place at the right time the day I met you." He kissed Mya passionately under the moonlight.

Seeing Antonio leave was one of the hardest things Mya had to do. Every one-more-last-kiss made it harder to say good bye. As a final goodbye Antonio kissed her on her forehead. "Baby, I have to go." He said and wiped a tear on her left cheek. Mya released him and he slowly walked away. She returned to Sarah's white dodge. "You alright?" Sarah patted her back. Mya nodded and wiped the tears.

Kim and Charles were getting ready for church. Kim was dressed in a black and blue pants suit. Diamond earrings glistened from her ears. Her curls were slightly pushed back by a thin headband. Charles wore a blue button down with a black and grey tie. With Aldo dress shoes at his feet. The two looked as if they came straight from a look book. "You ready?" Charles asked as he watched Kim dress her lashes with mascara. "Yes" She closed the bottle. Charles opened the car door for Kim and she slid in like a queen. He drove down the street to Dream Center Ministries.

"So remember that God is in control but you have to play your role as well. As a believer, as a child of God, as a warrior and not a worrier." The congregation clapped and hollered. "Know that our God is able! He will give us what we need when the time is right. Ecclesiastes 3:31 says He has made everything beautiful in its time. The only time we running on is God's" More clapping and cheering arose. The alter call music began. The sound of the piano played the tune to "I surrender all" softly. "Now, there may be somebody here today that needs prayer for the issues in their life. Don't let the devil discourage you from receiving the blessing that God woke you up and brought you here today to obtain. Please if you would like prayer today come to the alter now." Many people left their place to receive prayer. Charles squeezed Kim's hand. "No" She mouthed. Charles pulled Kim until her feet moved and they walked to the alter together. John and Catherine were in tears when they noticed Kim walking to the front. "We've been trying to get her to go for years." Catherine whispered to John. "I know. God is good." He pulled Catherine closer to him. "All the time" She sang to the music with tears streaming down her face.

Kim and Charles met up with her mother once service let out. They shared a warm embrace. "I'm so happy for you Kim." She kissed her cheek. "Thanks mom." Kim linked her arm with Charles. "Mom this is Charles." Charles extended his left hand. "Boy you better give me a hug." She joked. Charles hugged Catherine's petite figure. "It's such a pleasure to meet you." She grinned. "Likewise" The twins ran up and jumped on their mother. "MOMMY" They sang in unison. "Hi babies." She planted kisses all over their faces. "Mommy grandpa said you went to the front today!" Kimar shouted "Is it true mommy?" Kimora asked. "Yes it is." They hugged Kim tightly. When Kimar noticed Charles he leaped for joy. "Look Kimora its Mister Man" They hugged him. "Hey, Kimar! Hey, Kimora!" Kimar was out of breath. "Mister Man, did you go to the front too?" Charles nodded his head. "Dad, this is Charles" Kim presented Charles to John. "Pleasure to meet you Charles. Thank you for taking care of my daughter." John shook his hand strongly. "Let's go out for breakfast, my treat!" John suggested. "Mc Donalds!" The twins shouted. "How about Denny's?" John said. The twins danced out to the parking lot. Charles, Kim, and the twins sat in his car while Kim's parents tagged behind him.

Charles received a call from Antonio alerting him that he made it to Plainfield. They arranged to meet at a local bar.

"Thank you for coming. I'm sorry you had to cut your trip short." Charles said. "Man, my girl was a bit upset until she became my fiancée." Charles smiled. "Really? You popped the question my brotha?" Antonio smiled. "I had to man." Charles patted him on the back. "That's beautiful." He signaled the bartender. "Excuse me. Can we have two glasses of cognac please? The bartender nodded then prepared the drinks. "No" Antonio imposed. "I don't drink" Charles laughed. "It's a celebration. One won't hurt you." The bartender set the drinks in front of the men. Charles paid him. "Congrats" Charles raised his glass. Antonio tasted the cognac and found it wasn't too bad yet, one glass would be enough. Plus, he wanted to hear the news Charles had. "Tell me about the investigation." He anticipated a response from Charles.

"The day I called you was the same day Kim received news the police identified the men on the security tape. Unfortunately, they could not exchange the news over the phone. So Kim and I had to go to the station. That is when I called you. I wanted you to come with us." He sipped his drink. "Well, we got there and Kim changed her mind the instant we stepped foot in the building. But don't worry I talked her out of backing away. So, we meet the officers and they take Kim to the back room alone. She told me they showed her two photos of." Charles paused to finish his drink. "Mike and Jacob." Antonio's mouth met the floor. He picked up his drink finishing it completely. "Excuse me sir! Two more cognacs please."

"This is bad! Really bad." Antonio massaged his head. Charles let out a sigh. "I know Kim wants to sue the company." Antonio said, hoping Charles would say otherwise. Charles nodded. "Like hell."

"Why not Jacob and Mike? I mean they're the real criminals." He took a sip. "Think about it Charles, if she sues the company we could be out of a job. I can't afford that. You gotta talk her out of that."

Charles shook his head. "I don't know Antonio she is set on it."

Damn, if it aint one thing it's another. "Could you try?" Charles felt compassion for Antonio. "Yeah. I'll do what I can." Antonio paid the tab. "Thanks man." He headed out the bar.

Antonio sat in his car in disbelief. *Why did this have to happen at my job?* He could feel the liquor settling in his system. Able to drive he placed the black Porsche in gear and drove off. When he arrived home, the place was empty. *Great time to roll one.* He thought. He sat outside on the back patio. The sun was finally setting. The blue sky was drenched with the colors of orange and purple. It took his breath away. He wish he could hold Mya and watch the sunset just as they did in Carbondale. He wanted to make love to her one last time because the last time wasn't enough.

Chapter 17

Mya was so excited to pick up her ring from Kay Jeweler's that she ran into University Mall. "Hello!" She greeted Leslie upon her arrival. "Mya! Good to see you" Leslie could recognize her smile from miles away. "Is it ready?" Mya anticipated. Leslie nodded her head. "Give me a moment to get it for you." Leslie turned and walked to the back of the store to retrieve the ring. Mya waited patiently. Leslie returned with a black velvet box in her left hand. "Here you are." She passed over the box. Mya took it and then slowly opened the box falling in love with the ring all over again. "Yes!" She screamed. Mya placed the ring on her left finger, it was a perfect fit. She gazed at the ring and adored how it glistened in the bright lights at the store. "Thank you so much Leslie." She sang. "You're very welcome" Leslie flashed a smile. "Is there anything else I can help you with?" She asked. Mya shook her head. Leslie handed Mya a small purple bag. "In this bag there is cleaning supplies, a warranty for the ring, and a diamond certificate." Mya thanked Leslie again then headed out the door.

Once she got home, she called Antonio via skype. He answered on the first ring. Mya flashed the ring in the camera. "I got it, baby!" Her smiled glowed like the diamond. "It's beautiful, Mya." Antonio said. "Thank you, Antonio. I love it. I love you." She blew a kiss. "I love you" Antonio said not matching Mya's excitement. "What's wrong Antonio? Are you having second thoughts?" She asked afraid to hear his response. Antonio looked at Mya as if she stole something. "I'm going to pretend you didn't ask me that." He huffed. Mya rolled her eyes. "Well what is the problem?" She grew angry. "The case is driving me crazy." Mya felt compassion. "What happened? How did your meeting go?" She questioned. Antonio smiled. "I tried cognac for the first time." Mya laughed. "Baby, you don't drink."

"I know." He said, "It was for celebrating our engagement." Mya smiled liking the sound of that. Antonio continued, "I found out two men from my job are the perpetrators. Now the company is at risk. Kim wants sue, which means I could be out of a job." Mya shook her head. "Sorry to hear that baby." They sat in silence. Just then Luis came in Antonio's room and hopped on the bed. "Sup Antonio?" Antonio spoke with Luis for a moment until he noticed Mya on Skype. "Is that Mya?" He asked. "Hi Louie" Mya sang. Antonio tapped Luis on the shoulder. "Guess what?" He hinted for Mya to show the ring. "Look" He said pointing to the screen. Mya flashed her engagement ring. "You asked her to marry you?" He was in total shock. "And you said yes?" He asked Mya. She nodded. "That's cool." He said with his head facing down. "Does this mean I have to be nice to her now?" Antonio laughed. "Nah, you don't have to if you don't want to" Mya interjected. "That's bull!" She laughed. Antonio picked up the phone and blew her a kiss. "Baby, I'm fenna play with him. I'll talk to you later." Mya blew a kiss.

Chapter 18

"I'm only saying this because I respect Antonio." Charles wrapped his arms around Kim's waist. His strong chest covered her shoulders that now rested on him. They stood in the kitchen. "I respect Antonio too, but what happened there was inappropriate. I know it was not entirely his fault so suing the company is not fair to him. All I can say is that he was in the wrong place at the wrong time." Charles released her instantly. "Are you serious?" She turned to face him. Charles was appalled to see Kim nod her head. "What if someone said that to you Kim and your situation?" Kim slapped him across the face hard enough for blood to draw from his lip. "Fuck you Charles. Don't EVER compare what happened to ME to anything!" Charles held his puffed lip. He aimed a finger at her. "Keep your voice down you know the twins are sleeping." He said calmly. Kim rolled her eyes. *Now you're going to tell me not to yell in my house? Nigga, you trippin'* "You need to excuse yourself." She demanded. Charles sucked his bloody bottom lip. "You need to calm down." He trailed to the bathroom and covered a wet towel to his lip. Kim followed him. "Let me see" She said trying to inspect the wound. Charles nudged her off. Kim felt embarrassed for reacting in such manner. "I'm sorry." She mumbled. Charles remained silent attempting to maintain his patience. Once the bleeding stopped. Charles examined his lip, still puffy. "Let's get one thing straight about you and me." Kim looked up at him. "We will not put our hands on each other. Kimberly, if you do that to me ever again, I will leave you and never come back." Kim remained silent. Charles slightly lifted her chin up. "Do you understand?" "Yes" Kim said softly. Charles walked out the bathroom leaving Kim there. He lay on the bed watching late night TV.

Kim carefully stepped in the tub as the water ran for her bath. She rested as the bubbles formed and soon covered the entire tub.

Charles didn't understand why his gut feeling would not rest until he noticed the trail of water spilling through the crack of the bathroom door. *Oh GOD NO.* Charles rushed to the bathroom discovering Kim laying faced up in the tub. He stopped the water and cautiously removed Kim from the tub. He adjusted her body flat on the bedroom floor to begin CPR. After calling 9-1-1 Charles pushed to 30 compressions and gave 2 breaths praying mentally as he moved from compressions to breaths, breaths to compressions. After 5 cycles of doing this, Kim was still unconscious. "Damn it Kim. Come on! Don't die on me!" Charles was in tears. He hoped Kimora and Kimar had not been awakened. He knew it would kill them to see their mother in such a state. 10 minutes later EMS arrived. One attached an AED to her chest. "CLEAR" she announced. The rest of the EMT's stood back. Once the shock had been administered Kim's body ejected but she still had no pulse. They fixed her body on a stretcher and rushed her out of the apartment while the same EMT gave her CPR. Kimora and Kimar rubbed their eyes due to the bright lights coming from their window. "MOMMY!" Kimora shouted. The twins rushed out of their rooms to meet their lifeless mother on the stretcher. Kimar fell to the ground in tears. Kimora hugged him and said a prayer. Charles found the twins in that position, grateful God gave them strength to not panic. He wrapped his arms around them and they embraced him. Charles alerted Kim's parents and they all agreed to meet at the hospital.

Chapter 19

John, Catherine, Kimora, Kimar, and Charles were in constant prayer. In between times they sang a worship song. A male doctor with green eyes, caramel skin, and facial hair approached the hope filled family.

"Mr. and Mrs. Johnson?" He welcomed. John and Catherine stood to their feet and together greeted the doctor. He sympathetically gazed in their eyes. "I'm sorry, we did all we could." Catherine fell to the ground and John was in so much shock he could barely sustain her. From the sight of it all, Charles, Kimora, and Kimar had understood that Kim was gone. Kimar and Kimora ran to their grandparents. Charles quickly found a bathroom where he cried hysterically.

The doctors had informed Kim's parents that the cause of death was due to stroke that led to her drowning. "Would you all like to see her?" Catherine wiped the tears while nodding her head. John held Kimora at his side. "Let's go say goodbye to mommy." She rested her head wrapped in a silk scarf on John's shoulder. Catherine carried Kimar who embraced her tightly. "Where's Mister Man?" He asked. John looked at Catherine who shook her head. They continued walking. Upon entering through the door, the doctor paused to speak, "I would like to say I'm sorry for your loss, my prayers go out to this family. Your daughter fought hard but now she is at her time of rest. He opened the door allowing the family to go in.

Chapter 20

"I'm gonna kill them mutha fuckas!" Charles screamed in rage

"No you're not Charles. You're not going to kill them."

"Antonio, do not patronize me right now." Charles paced in the conference room.

Antonio sat with his legs crossed on the table. "Look Charles, I understand you're upset—"

"Furious Antonio, that's the word." He swung his fist across the air. "When I get my hands on them they're going to wish they were dead."

"Now you sound vengeful. I'm telling you Charles don't take this situation and create another black man goes mad report"

"It's too late for that. Them crackers messed with the wrong one." Charles punched the wall and instantly pulled back covering his face with tears. Antonio rushed toward him and stood as he watched Charles cry on his knees. Antonio shook his head. *God.* Soon as Charles was able to regain himself, he stood to his feet facing Antonio. Still fighting tears he spoke, voice trembling, "What am I supposed to do Antonio? Let them just take my woman like that? What if this was Mya?"

"I don't wanna think like that man?"

"You don't have to, I do and that's what you don't understand!" Charles walked out of the conference room swiftly heading toward the men's restroom.

Antonio entered the men's room finding Charles flushing his face with cool water. Charles sighed, turned off the water, and wiped his face with a paper towel. Once he caught a glance of Antonio's reflection, he turned and cocked his head to the left. "You came to spit more bullshit?" Antonio took a step forward, "Nah man, I came to say I'm down." He reached out his fist "Let's get them cracka fuckas." Charles sealed the deal with dap. They headed to the conference room in order to discuss a plan.

To be continued . . .

About the Author

G. I. WU is an aspiring writer from Saint Louis, Missouri. WU received a Bachelor's of Arts in Spanish from Southern Illinois University Carbondale. WU's inspiration stems from the injustices people of color are challenged with on a daily basis, relationships, and, faith. G.I. WU hopes to encourage readers to strengthen their faith in order to strategically overcome life's trials and to one day create a space for them to share their stories.